Cora Davis

Immortelles

Cora Davis

Immortelles

ISBN/EAN: 9783337377526

Printed in Europe, USA, Canada, Australia, Japan

Cover: Foto ©Andreas Hilbeck / pixelio.de

More available books at **www.hansebooks.com**

IMMORTELLES

BY

Mrs. CORA M. A. DAVIS

NEW YORK AND LONDON

G. P. PUTNAM'S SONS

The Knickerbocker Press

1887

PREFATORY NOTE.

This collection of the writings of Mrs. Davis was originally made with the intention of printing a volume simply for private distribution among relatives and friends, as a memento of her whom they had lost. In the belief, however, that the poems possess decided merit, it has been decided to place them before the public, which will, it is hoped, appreciate them at their true value.

The poems have been subjected to no revision or correction, but are printed exactly as they appear in the original manuscript. The editor cannot be certain that they are all in the final form which the author would have wished to give to them. This statement we beg the reader to bear in mind, that due allowance may be made for any inaccuracies.

A portion of the collection has been published before in various periodicals, but the majority of the poems now appear in print for the first time.

F. M. D.

IN MEMORIAM.

Cora M. A. Davis, the author of these poems, the daughter of William and Polly Bemis, was born in the town of Alabama, Genesee Co., N. Y., April 18, 1841. At an early age she removed with her parents to Waterford, Wis. Here her health suffered from malaria, which infected the locality at that time, and from which she never fully recovered.

At the age of six the family moved to a farm in the town of Center, Rock Co., Wis., where she remained until her marriage with F. M. Davis, Sept. 28, 1857. After residing in various places, Mr. Davis removed, in 1875, to Denver, Colo., where he still makes his home. Some years previous to this last removal, Mrs. Davis was attacked by Bright's disease, which terminated fatally Nov. 23, 1885.

Spending most of her life in the frontier States,

she learned to know and to love all that was beautiful and sublime in nature.

The grand old mountains, the dancing brooks, and the waving pines were her companions, and it was among these that her most beautiful poems were written. In the later years of her life, her mind seemed to dwell in realms remote from earth, and to delight in the scenes and associations of that beautiful "underworld" of which she sang. The fresh blooming Immortelles herein enshrined by loving hands, sacred to the memory of a faithful, loving wife and an idolized mother, were not written for the public eye, or intended for the ordeal of criticism, but are the breathings of a pure and exalted soul struggling for expression through the misty veil of mortality.

CONTENTS.

	PAGE
Prefatory Note .	iii
In Memoriam . . .	v
Earth's Fulfilment .	1
Down by the Sea	4
The Lover's Leap	11
Lenore . . .	15
To a Mountain Brook	21
The Snow-Slide . .	23
" He Doeth All Things Well "	27
Earth . .	30
Ruth . . .	38
A Dream within a Dream	53
The Song of the Brook	58
Pauline Grey .	61
Retrospection	66
Aphrodite	69
A Phantasy . .	72
We Will Seem to Forget . . .	74
Written for the Last Day of Professor W——'s School, 1876 .	77

	PAGE
A Storm in Midsummer	80
On the Moor .	84
Sea Mist	93
Proserpine	96
The Sea . .	102
I Come to Thee, O Nature!	105
Dream On, Young Heart	107
Hope . .	109
The Poor . .	111
Love and Primroses .	114
A Summer Pastime	116
Robin .	118
A Memory	119
A Kiss .	121
A Fragment	122
A Picture	125
A Secret .	127
Petrarch and Laura .	128
Time . .	129
A Dream	131
Ice-Bound	133
Haunted	134
Phantasma	137
Autumn	139
Lines Written to a Friend on the Fiftieth Anniversary of Her Birthday	141
A Vision	143

	PAGE
A Night . .	144
A Fragment of a Dream	145
A Summer in Dream-Land	146
To a Lost Thought .	147
Is There a Heart?	148
An Oasis	150
A Dream .	151
Water-Cresses	152
A Fragment	154
An Idyl .	155
On the Heights .	158
Snow .	159
To a Little Blue Flower	161
To ———	162
Written for the Last Day of Professor W———'s School for the Third Department. Motto on the Banner : "Upward and Onward"	164
Let Me Alone	166
A November Sunset . .	168
Midsummer	170
Lines Written in a Friend's Album	172
Drifting Leaves .	173
Sleep . . .	175
Growing Old (A Revery)	176

EARTH'S FULFILMENT.

A lofty mountain summit, pale and fair ;
Far-reaching heavenward, cleaving the blue air.
The misty distance wrapping it about
With mystery and charm ; that always, doubt
Of full possession, gives the unattained.

I watched it ; and by turns was joyed and pained
By its most changeful beauty.   Never dream
Held swifter flitting phantoms.   Now a gleam
Of sunset roses rested on its brow.
Now stern and cold, shrouded in spotless snow,
Distant and unapproachable it lay
Sleeping upon a cloud-draped couch of gray.
Sometimes with lowering brow, dark, blue, and cold,
And seeming to come nearer me, it frowned.
Again, with stately splendor-iris crowned—

I

Right regally it rose out of a sea,
Whose purple waves bore crests of burnished gold.
Half visible through dim cerulean haze,
Through long, lovely, indian-summer days,
Smiling afar off, tender, dreamily,
It ever as I looked seemed beck'ning me.
At length—borne on the passing waves of time—
I gained the summit of this height sublime.
I, who so oft ere this, in airy flight
Of fleet-winged imagery had climbed this height,
Now feared to lift my eyes, lest the full flood
Of Nature's beauty, bursting on me, should
Kill me with a mad excess of joy.   At last
With bated breath one eager glance I cast.
Around me wildly rolled an ashen sea
Whose vap'rous waves hid all of earth from me,
Save the cloud-girdled space on which I stood,—
A shoreless sea, a voiceless, filmy flood.

Somewhere beneath this moving mass of gray,
I knew the world that I had left must lay.

How far away, how like some fading dream,

Vague and unreal, did the old life seem.

It was as if unnumbered ages swept

Their mighty breath between, with all that slept

Therein.   Love, pride, and passion, joy, and woe,

Like phantom shapes, still, shadowy and slow,

Passed each in turn before my misty brain.

Softly from out the distance came a strain

Of solemn music, of a grand old song,

Touching my heart-strings as it swept along.

I cried : " Must thus the beautiful and bright

Just as we grasp them vanish from our sight ! "

And then—slow shaping in my mind—a thought

Was born ; that grew in beauty till it caught

The glory of a longed-for certainty.

A promise—as it seemed in words of gold

Written in every wind-waved filmy fold

Of the cloud sea—of immortality.

DOWN BY THE SEA.

One summer evening, down by the sea
I sat on the rocks and dreamily
  Watched the sea-weed drifting by.
That night the winds and waves were still ;
It seemed the power of some mighty will,
  So motionless, bade them lie.

I was tired of life that summer night ;
The things that once had given delight,
  Had lost all their charm for me.
Time had not fulfilled the hopes of youth,
Selfishly sordid and barren of truth,
  Life seemed but a mockery.

As I mused, I heard distinct and clear,
A deep, sad sigh ; to my startled ear

It seemed to come from the sea.
Listening, I heard again, and again,
A moan like a smothered cry of pain ;
   Each time sounding nearer me.

Then from the crystal waves of the sea
A sylph-like maiden rose silently,
   Seating herself at my feet.
To me she looked enchantingly fair.
Her foam-white arms and her feet were bare.
   Her glances were shy and sweet.

A robe as light as a morning mist—
Girdled with pearls at her slender waist—
   But half concealed her form.
A comb of coral, costly and rare,
Held the dusky gold of her waving hair.
   Her lips were rosy and warm.

She said : " I come from the coral caves,"—
Her voice had a sound of flowing waves,—

" I dwell with the mermaidens there,

But I am not one of their merry band,

I sigh for my people in far earth-land.

A garden sunlighted and fair.

" In other days, life's sunnier hours,

We dwelt amid the beautiful flowers,

Presiding o'er a fountain there.

And all day long, in frolicsome play,

I flung the glittering drops of spray ;

Giving each blossom a rightful share.

" Sometimes they fell in the chaliced gold

Of a queenly lily, chaste and cold ;

Sometimes in the heart of a rose.

Or I flung a shower of drops to wet

The thirsty lips of a violet ;

At a summer day's sultry close.

" There, mountains wrapped in a purple dream,

I saw through the fountain's silver gleam.

There, rose-flushed summer morn
Wore shimmering robes of golden mist,
The dewy edge of whose skirts I kissed
　When thousands of flowers were born.

" But mighty Triton came out of the sea
And wooed me and wished to wed with me.
　To wed him I would not consent.
My people, the great sea-god to please,
Hoping his fearful wrath to appease,
　Doomed me to endless banishment.

" And I forever down in the sea
Must dwell with the things that frighten me,—
　Slimy creatures that writhing move,—
Unless some mortal should wed with me,
And break the spell that enfoldeth me
　With the power of passionate love."

Her plaintive voice died away in sighs ;
A golden fringe drooped over her eyes,

As they sank beneath my own.
The white waves parted ; 'mid tossing spray,
My lovely sea-maiden glided away.
   I sat on the rocks alone.

Night after night, when the full moon shone,
I sat on the sea-beat rocks alone,
   Waiting, and listening, eagerly ;
But my fair sea-nymph was coy and shy.
She would not appear, would only sigh ;
   Though I pleaded most tenderly.

There came a time, 'ere the full moon waned,
The spirit of love unfettered reigned,
   And my foam-flower came to me.
Love broke the spell that enfolded her ;
With pledge and promise we wedded were,
   As the sun rose over the sea.

A crystal grotto close to the sea
Made fitting home for my bride and me,

Afar in a flowery land,—
A land with mountains of hazy gold,
A sunlit shore, forgotten and old,
　　By drowsy sea breezes fanned.

There by the blue waves' murmuring flow,
The sea and the mountain tops aglow
　　With the sunset's ling'ring red,
Of mosses white as the bleached sea-foam
And soft as the wool of a Persian loom,
　　We made our bridal bed.

On this quiet shore, unknown to sin,
Like lilies : " We neither toil nor spin,"
　　Yet are nourished by the sea.
We have no need of costly array ;
The sunny warmth of each summer day
　　Attires us right royally.

Better this dream-land a thousand-fold,
Than the world's sordid struggle for gold.

Better this life of leisure,
Than fruitless toil or wasting passion,
The world's unrest, its pride, its fashion,
Its cloy of selfish pleasure.

THE LOVER'S LEAP.

[Written on a mountain side in Colorado, at the foot of the
rocky cliff called "The Lover's Leap."]

This all-enduring, storied pile of gray,

Holdeth me by some strange fascination.

Here, on this lichen'd rock, close at its feet,

Refreshed by mountain breezes pure and sweet,

I 'll rest ; and yield me to the dreamy sway

Of Imagery.   Where, amid creation,

A fairer field for her unfettered flight,

Than here, upon this beauty-skirted height ?

Above me, skyward, towers the rocky steep ;

Beyond me, the illimitable sweep

Of distance ; there the city's far off gleam ;

Beyond, the plains, soft fading as a dream,

Farther and fainter, till the utmost edge
Of hazy purple—seen from this high ledge,
Wrapped in the distance—seems some shoreless sea
Upon the border of Eternity.

From far below, through balsam-breathing pine,
Come softened murmurs of the rivulet.
And plumy brakes, and tender ferns, enshrined
In mossy clefts, still linger in my mind.
The neighb'ring heights, through mists of azure
        shine
Like amethysts in bands of opal set.
And yet, without thine aid, O Imagery,
I might not feel the depths of the despair
That could have given birth to such a leap.
I fancy, looking on yon rocky steep,
That deep in cleft and crevice I can see
The trace of dark red stains still lingering there.

I pluck beside me from low growing bush,
Some leaves with crimson edges. Could it be

That in the death leap he had fallen here,
And stained the leaves with blood, and every year
When the new leaves appear—in memory—
They bear upon their edge this crimson flush?

I fancy, on that fatal hour 't was night;
And that the moon, full-orbed, a ghostly light
Shed on the scene; that that impassioned heart
Throbbed in a form of beauty, far apart
From common mortals; of a God-like size,
With thoughtful brow, and shadow-haunted eyes:
I seem to look into their depths; and there,
Read his love's unutterable despair.

I sit absorbed in dreamlike revery;
So real doth seem this past life's tragedy.
Only a moment passes, yet it seems
I 've wandered ages in a world of dreams.
One little wave of time the story told,
And all the while the sunshine's filmy gold
Plays o'er the leaves, the rocks, the daisy bloom

Low-lying at my feet.   Unchanged the scene
In outward seeming, yet a shade of gloom,
Invisible and undefinable,
The shadow of a shadow come between,
Saddens the spirit of the beautiful.

LENORE.

O'erlooking its rich, many-acred lands,
Grown gray with age, old Murry Castle stands
Its rock-invaded turrets, reaching high
Through lofty tree-tops, into the blue sky.
Below, through parted branches, gleams the sea ;
Beating against its gray rocks ceaselessly,
Laying its slimy sea-weed at their feet,
As murm'rous measures its dark waves repeat.

High on the castle's eastern side, a room
O'erlooked a gay parterre of bud and bloom ;
There, at the casement, Lady Lenore
Sat dreaming every day the same dreams o'er.
Dreaming, awhile the soft-rayed morning sun
Turned her flossy hair to wildering gold ;
Dreaming, awhile the mellow light of noon,

Lay warm in every sun-brushed, rippling fold ;
Dreaming, awhile the wan, white, lighted moon
Folded her in a mist, whose spectral gleam
Did make her fragile, white-robed figure seem
Some earth-bound, trancèd spirit, in a dream.

Always her eyes were fixed upon the sea ;
The sea, that gleamed, or purpled, as the light
Of sun, or shadow, held it changefully.
Watching, as if some long-expected sight
Must dawn upon her vision ; taking note
Of little else.   Each morn old Gretchen brought
Fresh dewy flowers for crystal-wrought epergne,
And rare old china vase, and silver urn,
Brought from o'er the sea ; and if by chance
Her Lady gave their beauty but one glance,
It was enough, old Gretchen was content.

With rosy silk, and rare old filmy lace,
The walls were hung in roseate folds that lent
A fairy-land's enchantment to the place.

Scattered everywhere in careless grace
Were things of curious beauty ; such as please
An antiquarian's æsthetic taste.
Upon the marble floor of the great room,
A carpet, wrought in some far Persian loom,
Where roses, fair as those of famed Cashmere,
With folded petals soft as silken floss,
Were sleeping upon beds of pale sea moss.

Only the sea, murmuring sad and drear,
Beating forever 'gainst its rock-girt waste
Of shore.   Only the sea, and one strange flower,
To please the Lady Lenore had power.
Always she wore a clinging robe of white ;
Some strange rich fabric, shimmering in the light,
And at her throat, amid the rare old lace,
She wore the flowers she loved, with tender grace.

So passed, in the slow passing time, each day ;
Save when " My Lord " came home for a brief stay.
And then arrayed in robes of rich brocade—

Whose folds held dusky shadows of old gold—
A picture fair to look upon she made
In the great banquet hall.   Each shining braid
Of her pale yellow hair with gems agleam,
She to " My Lord " most beautiful did seem.
And so he saw her thus, he questioned not ;
Or, if such question held his honest mind,
In kindly works of Charity he thought,
And such pursuits as gentle womankind
Are wont to love, his lady's life was passed.
And so no spirit of ill omen cast
Its vague foreshadowing across his way.

So time passed on, but there did come a day
Whose evening saw a great storm sweep the sea,
Lashing to foam the dark waves angrily.
With covered head, and lowly muttered prayer,
Old Gretchen crouched anear her Lady's chair,
Who at the casement, pale and sleeplessly,
Gazed affrighted toward the veilèd sea,
Then in the lightning's lurid glare she saw

A great ship struggling with the mad black waves.

Then through the roar, a crash, a fearful shock,

And the great ship was riven on the rock.

Reaching far through darkness toward the sea,

She cried : " My love, I 'm coming, wait for me."

A fall—the wild wind drowning the dull sound—

Ere this, unconscious Gretchen, weary, slept,

And darkness the night's dreadful secret kept.

Morn came ; and after a long search they found

The Lady Lenore all cold and dead

Upon the starry-blossomed odorous bed

Of the strange flowers she loved.   The sea

All passion-spent, its midnight mystery

Hiding beneath its white foam-crested waves,

With other mysteries of hidden graves.

They buried her beneath the tropic bloom,

And her bright garden and her silent room

Were closed, and no one ever entered there,

Save Gretchen, who with tender, jealous care

Tended the flowery grave, with prayers and tears,

Faithfully, through the long forgetful years.

My Lord, in foreign lands, absorbed in thought,

And scientific search, his loss forgot.

So, long-deserted, grim old Castle Murry

Became the prey of mildew and decay.

About it crept an air of mystery,

By superstitious servants fancies wrought,

By idle whispers, and by weird tales brought

To credulous listeners.   A phantasy

Of gliding spectres through the silent halls;

On nights of storm the sound of heavy falls,

Of moving lights along the lichened walls.

No charm had musty hall, or fireless hearth,

Or gloomy castle, or storm-beaten shore,

To woo the spirit of the Lady Lenore

Back to the scene of her life's discontent,

Its wasted years of weary waiting.

That night of storm was one of joyful meeting.

Somewhere beyond the shadows of this earth,

Her soul had found at last peace and fulfilment.

TO A MOUNTAIN BROOK.

O beautiful rock-prisoned stream !
Offspring.of the snow-crowned mountain,
You fret, that the passive rocks seem
Your swift, wayward course to restrain.
But fret, plunge, and foam as you may,
Break your bright waves in your anger,
There, cold and unmoved, in your way,
Still lies the passionless bowlder.

Here on this gray rock of ages,
Alone 'midst turbulent waters,
I hear, it seems, many voices ;
A chaos of elfin murmurs.
Around me white foam-wreaths are flung ;
I know, in a vague, dreamy way,

—Though they speak in an unknown tongue—
What the eerie water-sprites say.

Though they pelt me with spray, and mock,
Those elves of the wild, mountain stream,
Content and secure on my rock,
I sit here for hours and dream ;
And follow the shadows that play
O'er the gold of the cañon walls,
Till the gold melts into the gray,
And a soothing spell o'er me falls.

The tangle of thoughts in my brain
Smooths out in definite way ;
Half forgotten the shadow of pain,
And a soft rose flushes the gray.

THE SNOW-SLIDE.

The duskiness of winter's early night
Is on the mountains.   From a clear cold sky
A few pale stars—dimmed by the ling'ring light—
Shine feebly.   Valley, rock, and mountain high,
Are covered deep with white, unbroken snow.

Along a narrow road a mountaineer
And heavy laden mule are plodding slow
And sturdily ; both man and beast appear
Roughened by winds, and storms, and wintry days,
Hardy toil, and long, and perilous rides.
They know but little of life's flowery ways ;
Save, as spring blossoms on the mountain sides.

A shaggy bear-skin coat—well worn and warm,
Girded about the waist with leathern belt—
Envelops close the hunter's brawny form.

His head protected by a tawny felt,
Beneath whose slouching brim keen eyes peer out
From heavy brows above a frosty beard ;
Restless, suspicious eyes that glance about
With furtive watchfulness, as if he feared
Some object might escape them ; eyes that speak
Of courage, and of strength.   With steady stride,
Measured and firm, the drifted snow he breaks,
His patient pack-mule plodding at his side.

What means this silence that stealthily
Hath come upon the night ; not even a breath
Of wind sweeps through the pine trees, drearily
Sighing through drooping branches.   Only Death
Or Sleep, deep and dreamless, hath such silence.
Or, is it the hushed calm foreshadowing
Some dread event, when Earth, in rapt suspense,
Breathless, seems waiting what the hour may bring ?

Something of this—in fancy undefined,
Rude and unshaped, the shadow of a fear—

Is in the sturdy mountaineer's mind.

He pauses, listening, as it were, to hear

Some unaccustomed sound ; a sound to break

The deep prophetic stillness of the night.

And now, he sees, with senses all awake,

Far down the curving road a gleam of light.

Low on the mountain side it feebly gleams.

To him this light means food and warmth and rest ;

Aye more, for rough and hardened as he seems,

A voiceless love abideth in his breast.

Within the cabin rude, whence streams the light,

His father, wife, and fair-hair'd daughter wait.

In fancy now he sees—O cheering sight ! —

The savory evening meal beside the grate.

But hark, what is this low and threatening sound—

Like muffled thunder—breaking on the night.

With terror-startled eyes he looks around

To see a shapeless moving mass of white,

A pallid, hungry monster, weird and wide,

Rushing and crashing down the mountain side ; —
A little way below his cabin stands.
With wild, dilated eyes, and powerless hands,
Speechless, he watches the relentless foe,
Destroying all before it, downward sweep.
A moment, and his home lies fathoms deep,
Buried beneath a trackless field of snow.

With one deep groan, he frees from heavy load
His frightened mule, and mounting, hastens back ;
Urging the weary beast with spur and goad
O'er the drifted, perilous, mountain track ;
Shouting for help ; onward with frantic leap ;
On, for nearest aid ; vain undertaking.
Ere help can reach them they must surely sleep
The sleep of death ; the sleep that hath no waking.

"HE DOETH ALL THINGS WELL."

Unto all lives must come some darkened days ;
When all too long and barren, seem life's ways ;
When heaven seems a myth, so far away
That e'en far-reaching hope sees not a ray
Of light through the impenetrable gray,
Veiling its glory from all mortal eyes.

When such a shadow darkens life's dull sky,
Turn thou to nature's restful solitude ;
Deep in the heart of some still, sun-brushed wood
There, in some lovely, shade-enfolded nook,
Close to the grassy brim of some clear brook,
Throw yourself down upon the fragrant sod,
And let your thoughts soar upward, nearer God.

27

I cannot tell what soothing, restful power,
Lies in the beauty of each woodland flower,
In the languorous murmurs of the brook,
In dreamy music by the free winds shook
From quiv'ring leaves against an azure sky.
Look upward through the swaying branches ; high,
And higher, into the deep, shimmering blue.
Soon every doubtful shadow haunting you
Will fade, and vanish into nothingness.

And soothed as by some holy tenderness,
It seems some mighty arms your soul uplifts,
Higher and higher, till, through shining rifts
In heaven's close-drawn veil of mystery,
You catch some strains from that grand symphony
Of the eternal life ; a rhythm divine
Will linger in your soul throughout all time.

Thus, folded close to nature's throbbing heart,
You feel yourself to be of God, a part ;
And bound by laws immutable, to be

A perfect cord in life's grand harmony.

Cherish this prophecy within your breast ;

Be brave and true, and leave to God the rest.

Cease, weary heart, to struggle and rebel ;

Be patient, wait, He doeth all things well.

EARTH.

Let 's sing the beauties of this grand old earth,
Rolling with endless rhythm through endless space,
Her heart, a sea of surging liquid fire,
Her surface, home of the great human race.
With precious stones and mineral wealth between
Her heart of fire and crust of living green.

While fossils deep embedded in the stone,
True records, read by geologic lore,
Prove that this planet world had been the home,
Of man, ages and ages gone, before
Frail woman, as tradition doth aver,
Gave to man the knowledge he boasts of now.

Her ocean's phosphorescent, crested waves,
Their depths concealing curious life and mystery

Of coral reefs, and graves.

Hiding 'mong shells and tangled plants a history ;

Her everlasting mountains, crowned with snow,

Grow purple, seen from valleys green below.

What glowing grandeur in the silent wilds,

Where mighty gorge, and yawning chasm divides

The rocky hardness of the towering piles

Of cliffs, which winds for ages have defied ;

Their shadowy sides of gray each traced across,

With feathery arabesques of clinging moss.

'T were vain to try to paint the sunset's gold,

Fleec'd with crimson, purple, amber lights,

The solemn hush that broods o'er eventide,

The loveliness of moonlit summer nights,

The dewy purity of early morn,

Or fragrance of young, dewy buds, night-born.

Her silent forests, solemn, grand, and old.

Bathed in perpetual shade, save when

Some wandering sunbeam, tinging all with gold,
As if scared by the shadows, vanishes again,
An instant flashing through, and then away,
Leaves but a transient, quivering, golden ray.

These giant trees, their trunks all mossy gray,
Draped with wild grape, and clinging ivy vines.
There pale wood orchids droop their starry spray,
And scarlet honeysuckle grows, and wild woodbine,
And fragile milk-white lilies, bending low,
Kiss mossy banks, where fringing fern-leaves grow.

Modest wood violets, and blue forget-me-nots,
Waxen lady's-slipper, and creepers snowy white,
And pale wild roses haunt the loveliest spots,
While graceful wild birds flit with plumage bright,
Where brown cupped acorn-clusters pendent swing,
'Mong polished oak-leaves, there their sweet notes
　　　ring.

Her pebbly bottomed brooks, with willows fringed,
Whose limpid waters through green meadows flow,

Upon whose rippling surface creamy water-lilies lay,

Along whose grassy margin yellow cowslips grow,

Where in the drooping willow branches, all day
long,

Is heard the red-winged blackbird's liquid note.

Earth's lovely lakes on her fair bosom lay,

Like great translucent opals, in emerald frame ;

Her azure tinted rivers go murmuring on their way,

Their mournful, rushing music ever the same ;

While waterfalls in nature's loneliest by-ways,

Pour down their misty columns of rainbow-tinted
spray.

Her flashing geysers, her ice-bound polar seas,

Where icebergs cold, reflect the weird auroral lights ;

Her crystal grottos, and her spar-lined caves,

With lofty chambers, glittering with pendent stalac-
tites ;

A winter morn, arrayed in frosty white,

Transformed to magic beauty by the first moonlight.

The balmy spring days, when the robin comes,
And the air is sweet with the scent of blooming
    clover ;
When broods of downy chickens first behold the
    sun,
And on the hill-side blooms the first spring flower ;
When wild birds choose the mate they love the best,
And with hopeful twitterings, together build a nest.

Her summers with reign of fragrant roses,
The blushing glory of the golden days,
Gay autumn's orchards with their ripe fruits heavy ;
The sighing winds and veil of purple haze ;
The changing brilliancy of falling leaves,
The spell that, 'round all, indian-summer weaves.

The tropics, wrapped in Oriental splendor,
And languor born of dreamy lotus flowers,
The gorgeous cactus bloom, the wreathing mistletoe,
The groves of palms, and death-hued cypress bow-
    ers,

Where soft winds, in their wanton wanderings
    ceaseless,
Laden with spicy odors, woo forgetfulness.

The architectural beauty which her cities wear,
Their halls of music, and fine sculpturing,
Their frescoed galleries of rare old paintings, where
Is seen the work of hands long mouldering
To dust ; the mellow richness of whose tints im-
    part,
By contrast, greater delicacy still to modern art.

We tread in silence through her grand cathedrals,
Whose sculptured beauties centuries have wrought ;
Gaze with awed spirit down labyrinths of twilight,
That from the windows crimson hues have caught,
And reverence, spite of reason's admonition,
These mossy thrones of ignorant superstition.

Imagination paints old Egypt's former glory,
Of mighty temples reaching heavenward,

Of grim, colossal statues, whose barbaric story
The caustic pens of erudition still record,
Whose ancient cities of glittering minarets
Reflect the gold of Afric's gorgeous sunsets.

But standing now above her ancient cities,
All drifted in with golden desert sands,
One sees her temples ruined, her sepulchres long
    broken,
Her mighty people a few wandering bands ;
Sees where the mighty treacherous sands are drift-
    ing fast,
And sighs that earthly beauty cannot last.

From science's depths, to our astonished vision,
Daily some new discovered truth is brought ;
From books, and nature's close investigation,
Daily we glean new food for thought ;
Oh ! life were worth the living, if in its comple-
    tion
We could but fathom the mysteries of creation.

To write of all earth's beauties we behold,

Would take more than the life to man decreed,

Fore ere we 've written half the old, new truths unfold.

If heaven is fairer than our earth, 't is fair indeed.

Thus, seeking to know more of earth, on would we
drift.

The veil of mystery that enfolds her, time alone
can lift.

RUTH.

The autumn days had come upon the earth,
And pendent clusters purple grew, and mirth,
Soul of the grape, attained a mellow richness
In the golden sunshine of the indian-summer,
Whose hazy veil hid with its folds the distance,
And laid its dreamy spell upon earth's children.
The sighing autumn winds bred a "sweet melan-
    choly"
In nature's bosom, sweet, subdued, and holy ;
As we some fancied sadness nurse within our
    hearts,
And feel a depth of sweetness in the pain ;
As we, to hide the grief deep in our hearts,
Assume a careless gayety we do not feel.
So Autumn deck'd herself in her gay robes

To hide from earth the sadness of her spirit.

A chill wind, wandering restlessly about,

Whispered to the flowers of the coming winter ;

They listened, grew pale, withered, and died,

And the frost - touched, gorgeous - tinted autumn
leaves

Silently falling, covered o'er their graves.

The birds took airy flight to summer climes,

And frosty fingers scattered the ripe nuts

In showers down to the ground, among the
leaves,

And troops of rosy children gathered them

To add to winter evening's greater cheer.

Later, a keen wind whistling through the cornfield,

Rustling crisp husks that clasped the golden ears,

Drove wildly, here and there, the first white snow-
flakes,

And tinged the farmer's nose and ears with red,

As he, with busy fingers, heaped the baskets up,

To swell the pile that lay in the big barn,

Ready for the merry huskers, the coming night.

Within the old red farm-house, whose low eaves
Sheltered a row of hanging swallows' nests,
The farmer's broad-faced wife, with sleeves rolled
    up,
And blue-checked apron, tied about her waist,
Stood by the blazing fire, with fork in hand,
Turning the crisp doughnuts in the bubbling fat ;
While pretty, buxom Sally beat to frost the eggs,
And made and baked the golden pumpkin pies ;
And slender Ruth, with the dark, dreamy eyes,
And broad white forehead, dusted the best room,
And filled the china vases on the mantelpiece
With dark, rich, autumn leaves, and bright-red
    berries ;
Singing the while, with a sweet, plaintive voice,
The quaint words of an old familiar hymn.
Her thoughts, the while, divided were, between
The maple leaves and the night's festivities.
Down in her heart a sweet hope fluttering,
That thoughtful David would be there, and she
Might sit beside him at the husking bee.

The doughnuts fried and heaped up in pans,

And flaky crusted apple pies, and spicy mince,

In tempting rows, were ranged upon the shelves ;

And cookies scolloped and heart-shaped, fragrant
    with

Caraway seed, crisp and tender were, and plen-
    tiful ;

And shining pans, heaped high with juicy pears ;

And apples, ripe and mellow, crimsoned cheeked ;

And rich old cheese in generous slices cut,

Dried beef and pickled cucumbers, and all

The good things that New England pantrys boast

Of, when there is to be a husking bee at night.

The kitchen floor was scoured and neatly sanded,

And every thing in tidy order placed, and both

The burnished candlesticks new candles held.

The barn was lighted up, the floor swept clear,

And John and Reuben dressed in their best suits

Already were, and eager for the evening's frolic.

The candles in the parlor lighted were,

And the farmer's wife, arrayed in gay delaine

And silk cravat, in a stiff straight-backed chair,
In state, expectant sat ; while the good farmer,
His cue all nicely braided, in the warmest corner
Of the kitchen, sat smoking his pipe ; and all was
    ready
But the girls, who, in their room above, were each
Lending a sisterly helping hand to dress the other.
Sally, in a close-fitting dress of sapphire blue,
Squeezed her plump form, and curled her yellow
    hair.
And dark-eyed Ruth, with a sky-colored ribbon,
Banded it back, and pinn'd her snowy collar ;
Her own lithe form, arrayed in rosy crimson,
Her dark hair coiled in heavy, glossy braids,
'Mong which was twined a spray of scarlet berries.

The little, narrow gilt-framed mirror
Reflected first the black hair, then the yellow,
As they, as pretty women will, with magic touch
Adjusted here a braid and there a curl, and cast
Sly looks of admiration at their own sweet faces.

The scraping sound below of heavy boots,

A loud " haw haw," and hearty " how de do ";

And Sally, with a blush, cried " Jonathan 's come,"

Taking a last look, tripped lightly down the stairs.

And Ruth, a little smile curling her scarlet lips,

Saw, in her mind, the tall loose-jointed figure,

Bowing at the door with flourishing effrontery ;

His straight, tight locks cut close, and pasted
    down

With oil that strongly smelled of wintergreens ;

His striped vest of red and yellow hue,

His blue-black coat, the waist a trifle short,

A pair of red pumps peeping from the pocket.

Jonathan, whose good nature and easy, careless
    swagger

Made him a favorite with half the country girls ;

Jonathan, the petted favorite of all the mammas,

For, owned he not the nicest farm about ?

Jonathan, happy in a good opinion of himself,

And next himself, a good opinion of his friends.

Still, loath to go, Ruth, listening, lingered.

Her thoughts went wandering back, and hovered
    o'er
One moonlit, summer night, as a humming-bird
Hovers over the honey cup of a fragrant lily.

One moonlit summer's night when she and David
Had wandered down the lane, all over-hung
With apple boughs, whose drift of rosy bloom
Perfumed the summer night air with their breath.
Only four months ago, and yet, so long, it seemed
More like a sweet fragment of a dream, than like
    reality.
A wild rose growing by the wayside she had picked,
On whose pink petals night had left a tear,
And he, his blue eyes full of a sweet meaning,
Had asked her for the rose, and she had given it
    him.
And all the months that he had been away,
Sweet hope had nestled in her heart, and with
Its light, made radiant every hour of every day.
And she had built a rose-hued castle on the frail

Foundation of a dewy wild rose, and a tender look.

But now, to-night, doubt, like a tiny speck,

Rose in the clear horizon of her maiden dreams,

And fed by thought, grew larger, till it hid

Her fairy, rose-hued castle in its darkness.

Perhaps four months of city life had changed him,

Perhaps he had forgotten that moonlit summer
    night,

And had not kept the wild rose she had given him.

Some other heart than hers, perhaps, had thrilled

Beneath the tender glances of his eyes.

O silly Ruth, to build your love-lit castle

On a dewy wild rose, and a tender look.

But hark ! that quick, firm step was surely his ;

That deep voice, greeting them, she knew too well,

Be still, poor silly heart, for your wild throbbing

May wake no answering thrill in David's heart.

But though 't were so, no look or tone of hers

Should e'er betray the misery she was feeling.

With head thrown proudly back, her pale cheek
    flushed,

Her dreamy eyes lit up with a strange fire,
Her scarlet lips just slightly curled ; she looked
A very queen, as she, descending, met him,
And greeted him politely, as she did the rest, altho'
Her heart was fluttering, as she met his eager eyes
Bent on her with the same old look of tenderness
They wore that summer night, under the apple
    boughs.
Then turning, with strangely inconsistent manner,
To Jezekiah, an awkward country youth,
Lavished sweet, bewildering smiles upon him,
Seeming oblivious to every one but him ; though
Seated at his side among the merry huskers
Who clustered 'round the pile of yellow ears,
Many a furtive peep, from under her long lashes,
She stole at fair-haired David, o'er the pile—
Noting how well his stylish clothes became him,
How manly he had grown while he had been away.
And, though she seemed absorbed in Jezekiah,
Her listening ear caught every word he uttered,
And every answering smile he gave to Jennie Gray,

The pretty, blue-eyed girl who sat beside him,

She saw, with heart-felt pangs of jealousy.

And David, though he seemed to see her not,

Flashed angry fire from his eyes at Jezekiah ;

Found a red ear and strove for his reward.

At last the corn was husked, and snugly heaped

In the clean bins ; the husks all cleared away ;

And the violins gave out the enlivening strains

Of Opera reel, and stirring Money musk ;

And Jonathan, who, 'mong a crowd of maidens,

Was sitting, lordly, as a cock among his hens,

Rolling his great eyes, first to one side, then the
    other,

With gratified self-love and consequential manner,

Chose pretty Sally from among the group,

And was the first upon the floor to dance.

David looked eagerly at Ruth, and started toward
    her,

But she, appearing not to see him, gave her hand

To Jezekiah, who bore her off in triumph.

Thus merrily the hours went flitting by, till

The pale light of morn, appearing in the east,

Warned them that the night was passed ; and so

The good-nights all were said, and David went

Without a parting word.   But Ruth took comfort

In the hope that she would see him on the morrow.

But when the morrow came, though she watched
    eagerly,

And started when she heard the opening gate,

He came not that day, or the next, nor yet the next.

And thus the days went slowly by, till only one

Lay 'twixt that and the day of his departure.

With wild regret, and slowly fading hopes,

Ruth thought as she awakened in the morning :

" This is the last day of his stay ; oh ! shall I see
    him,

Or will he leave me without even a good-bye ? "

She rose and drew apart the snowy curtains

That draped the little window of their room.

And lo ! a white frost, with its feathery wreathings,

Lay still on every leaf, and twig, and bough ;

While through the frost-draped forest trees

The atmosphere imparted to the distance

That pale blue tint of color it only wears

On these rare, first wreathed winter mornings.

Innate with Ruth was a love for the beautiful,

And now she stood there, gazing as if spell-bound,

Drinking in the soft enchantment of the scene ;

Her long hair floating in black waves about her,

Her snowy night-gown loose and scarce concealing

The little rose-tipped feet on the cold floor.

Then, seized with keen desire to view the valley

From the wooded hill-side, just beyond the brook,

Hurriedly she dressed, and coiling up her heavy hair,

Tied on a pretty, black-silk hood with scarlet lining,

Wrapping herself in the soft folds of a scarlet cloak,

Tripped lightly down the stairs, and down the lane,

And took the little path that led across the brook

And up the wooded hill-side, leaving, as she went,

A row of tiny tracks in the thin, frozen crust

Of snow that carpeted the earth with white ;

And scarcely paused till, high upon the hill,
She turned to view the glorious scene below ;
Her great, dark eyes, all radiant with appreciation
Of this most beautiful of nature's scenes.
Far east and west stretched the lovely valley,
A little ice-bound brook winding along its length,
O'er which a fringe of feathery willow branches,
Heavy with glittering frost, drooped low.
Adown the rocky banks, adorned with frosty fringe,
The grand old forest trees towered up
Their white forms 'gainst the clear, blue sky.
With magic touch, had nature's skilful fingers,
In one short night, woven this delicate web
Of frostwork, to deck her daughter, earth,
For the morn's reception of the rising sun.
And lo ! just now, as all in white arrayed,
Scarce breathing lest her drapery be disturbed,
She waits expectant, fair as fairyland's
Enchantment. One flashing, golden glance the sun
Sends down upon her, and great rose-hued clouds
Of blushes flush the clear opal of her sky,

And every tiny crystal of the rare embroidery

Of her robe glitters like precious stones, beneath

The dazzling brilliancy of his first warm glance.

Ruth, standing with clasped hands and swelling
    heart,

Looked upon the earth thus glorified, and felt

Her whole soul full of worship for God,

So near her in that moment's inspiration.

A step in the crisp snow, and turning, she beheld

David, a gun upon his shoulder, his beard

All white with frost, his face aglow with the same

Enthusiasm that lighted hers. At sight of him, her
    love,

Rebellious. rose, and there, so close to nature and
    to God,

She could not hide it with the mask of coquetry ;

So, with her love all shining in the depths

Of her dark dreamy eyes, with quick impulsive
    movement,

She toward him turned ; he, looking in her eyes,

Clasped her close to him, whispering eagerly :

" You love me, Ruth, as I love you, my darling.

I read it in your eyes as you turned toward me,

And here, with glorious nature for a witness,

I offer you my hand, my heart, and the great love

That has been growing stronger all the years

Since we were children, till it has become

Of me, my life, my very being a part."

A light wind, playing among the branches,

And shaking the white frost down upon the snow,

Caught up her whispered answer, and repeating it

To every frost-gemmed spray and rose-hued cloud,

Wafted it to heaven ; where, as the love of the two
  souls

Blended in perfect harmony, a rapturous chord

Of music thrilled through all the spheres,

And woke a trembling echo from the earth—

Rejoicing of the angels at the pure uniting

Of two souls destined by creation for each other.

A DREAM WITHIN A DREAM.

I sit here alone with the night,
Alone in this grand ghostly room,
And the gleam of this flickering light
But adds to the shadowy gloom.
Without, the wild blast moaneth high
In the tree tops, that shivering groan,
And the dead leaves hurrying fly,
And the last pale flowers with a moan,
Droop their beautiful heads and die.
I know, past the sound of my call,
There is life in the servants' hall ;
But what are they, sleeping, to me
In my strange waking misery ?
Could I help, when I heard that night
My Lady lay ill at the Hall,

My heart gave a thrill of delight
That I should inherit it all ;
All, all, of this princely estate,—
For I am the nearest of kin.

O God ! is there blood on my hands ?
I fancy I see everywhere
(At thought of my castle and lands)
Those eyes with their dull, glassy stare.

I will sleep, and sleeping forget,
In this bed where a king might repose.
I draw back the rich tapestry
With its quaint flowers of dusky gold,
I turn down the silk coverlet
With its silver embroidery,
And the linen, whose every fold
Is sweet with the scent of the rose.

I sink in a languor to rest,
In the down of the wild swan's breast.
Can I never shut out that grave
Where the long dank grasses wave,
In a wind that moans and complains,

And curdles the blood in my veins ?

Do I wake, or is it a dream ?

I see in the cold, pallid gleam

Of the dawn, through the open door,

A pale shape glide into the room.

How noiselessly over the floor

It moves ; crouching close to the wall,

As it fades away in the gloom !

There, there, in the shadowy light

It is ; wan and rigid and white !

Its hollow eyes fixed upon me,

As moving, close, close to the wall,

It stealthily creeps toward my bed.

Its eyes are the eyes of the dead.

If its hand should clutch at my heart

With its cold death grip, I should die.

In a frenzy of horror, I start

From my bed with a stifled cry.

Thank God it is only a dream.

I am here in my simple room.

The grandeur, the horror, the gloom,
Have vanished away with the night.
Through the window the morning light
Comes in with a comforting gleam ;
And with it, a sweet wind that blows
The breath of the hawthorn and rose.

A messenger sent from the Hall
Brings tidings.   My Lady will live.
How light is my heart, as I give
True thanks, She is welcome to all,
To all of her princely estate.
I am young, I can work, I can wait.
'T is better to bring to my wife
The peace of an innocent life,
Than a burdensome title and lands,
With the shadow of blood on my hands.

I hear the birds sing in the hedge.
Was ever so lovely a morn ?
The sun gilds the blue mountain ledge,

It seemeth the earth is new born.

I pause by a dew-laden bough,

I swear by the soft wind that blows,

I never, no never, till now,

Found such sweets in the heart of a rose.

THE SONG OF THE BROOK.

On a wooded hill-side deep in shade,
A granite rock has for ages laid,
 And dark and gray its sides have grown
'Neath the touch of passing centuries,
And lichen and moss wove fantasies
 In arabesques of gold and brown.

From this gray rock's creviced breast I spring ;
And drop by drop, with a tinkling ring,
 Into the hollowed cup of stone
I fall ; and deepen the mimic lake,
That every passing breeze doth shake ;
 Then, leaping over, ripple down
Under the boughs of the elder bush,
Where the dappled wing of wild brown thrush

Flits in and out with restless whir.

Silently on through the darksome shade,

By tangled ivy and brier made,

    I flow, and sleepy ferns scarce stir.

'Neath the red and gold of a woodland plant

That catches the sunbeams shot aslant,

    I ripple on in a careless way ;

And flash my jewels, and gayly trill

A merry song, and quiver and thrill,

    Bending the rushes in wanton play.

Plashing along with a murmur low,

I pass where the lovers' flower doth grow,

    And as I pass the dreamy spot,

Though this flower blue is coy and shy,

I catch a glance from its starry eye,

    And the whisper—For-get-me-not.

I eddy and whirl where bowlders lay ;

I creep round cresses crisp, in my way,

And linger where lilies bend to drink

From twilight nooks, whose shadowy gloom

Is brightened by the azure bloom

    Of violets close to the brink.

I catch the green leaves' emerald lights,

Or the dusky gloom of summer nights,

    As I flow to the purple sea.

I bear on my breast the petals white

Of a sweet wild rose—a burden light

    The summer wind hath given me.

O sunny willows that shelter me,

O airy birds that warble for me,

    O meadows flecked with the cowslip's gold,

Where glances sly I flash as I pass

At strawberries hid in the tall lush grass!

    O beauty that wandering brooks behold!

PAULINE GREY.

Pauline Grey had eyes of azure ;
Full of youthful, sparkling pleasure ;
Though her life to slowest measure
    Moved.
Naught she knew of pride or fashion,
Social strife or sinful passion,
Though she—learning love's first lesson—
    Loved
Robert Leigh, a stout young farmer,
Manly, sun-burnt, quite a charmer
Said the maidens, so said rumor,
So thought Pauline Grey.
And all through one lovely summer
They had listened to the murmur
Of love's voice ; passing together

Idle hours away ;

Wand'ring through the fragrant meadows

Where the purring, grass-brimmed brook flows ;

Lingering when the twilight shadows

Veiled the sleeping day.

Came there from a neighb'ring city

One, was blasé, handsome, witty ;

Who had wealth unbounded—pity

Robert Leigh.

Saw he her with eyes of azure,

And her beauty gave him pleasure ;

All his many hours of leisure

Wooed he her.

Often in the moonlit evening,

Wandered they ; her mind receiving

New ideas wondrous pleasing.

Told he her

Of the world's impassioned measure,

Of its giddy whirl of pleasure,

And the charm of wealth and leisure.

Whispered he—

And his voice was low with passion—

That arrayed in garb of fashion,

Gems, her neck and arms a-flash on,

She would be

Fairer than the very fairest.

Would she wed him, he would cherish

Her forever ; sweetest, dearest,

Love's first dream.

Then she promised ; by wealth's glare

Blinded, dazzled.   On her fair

Slender hand a solitaire

Was a-gleam.

'T was the night before her wedding.

In the garden's dusky gloaming

Pauline walked ; pensively dreaming,

All alone.

Dreaming of the world's great splendor,

Lordly palaces and grandeur.

Of the old love true and tender,

Heedless grown.

Smiles played in her soft cheeks' dimple ;

Dressed was she in white robe simple ;

On her bosom, lay sweet, purple,

Clustered violets.

Fair will she look at her wedding

In her shimmering robe of satin,

Yet, withal, is vaguely dreading

Though she love forgets.

Later grows the charmèd hour ;

And the fragrance of each flower

Wooes her heart with its old power ;

Suddenly,

Young Robert Leigh stood at her side

All passion-spent and gloomy-eyed.

" You have broken my heart," he cried,

" Pauline Grey."

Then he caught the violet spray

That on her throbbing bosom lay

And kissed them wildly, tenderly,

Flung them scornfully away,

And was gone. Full of regrets,

Torturing, passionate regrets,

She found the broken violets,
Laid them tenderly away.

Swift years pass ; and Pauline Grey
Over her world of fashion gay
Holdeth unrivalled, queenly sway.
Young and old
Rave about her wondrous beauty ;
Of her passionless, cold beauty,
Of her air patrician, haughty
Red lips curled.
Of her dark-fringed shadowy eyes,
Deep within whose azure lies
Unuttered sadness that defies
All her world.
Within a silken-lined casket,
With neither gold nor jewels set,
She hides her withered violets
From the world.

RETROSPECTION.

To-night my thoughts go straying through the years
Back to the old farm-house again.
Along the road the quiv'ring poplar rears
Its stately head.   With sudden pain
I see the rambling house—low-roofed and gray—
Amid the locust's deepening shade,
Under the charmed spell of harvest laid.
'T is afternoon of a midsummer day ;
And drowsy silence broods the scene.
Upon the doorstep—worn by beating rains,—
Midway atween the twin rose trees,
Whose crimsoned branches sweep the window panes,
And fling upon the languid breeze
Their spicy incense—I will dream again,
As in the olden days I dreamed

Through long charmed hours of idleness; and when,
Like opening fairy-land, earth seemed ;
When life, like some vague, sweetest mystery,
Far in the smiling distance lay,
And with soft, luring promise, beckoned me
To time's fulfilment, fair alway.

From golden fields of grain the whirring sounds
Of harvest reaping come to me.
Across the road, the groups of grassy mounds
Appear an undulating sea.
I see the garden's tangled wilderness
Of leaves and flowers ; there in the shade,
Are tender blossoms sweet and colorless, ·
And violets past limits strayed,
And morning-glory vines that trail
Their rose and azure o'er the currant bushes,
And may-pink borders shorn and pale,
That every May with crimson flushes.
There, clumps of phlox, whose snowy-clustered
    bloom,

Like spectres robed in ghostly white,
Gleamed athwart the dusky, shadowy gloom
Of soft, star-lighted, summer nights.
'Long the quaintly bordered walk I loiter,
To see what buds morn shall unfold,
'Mong roses, pansies, spicy pink, and larkspur,
And tiger-flowers with cups of gold,
And purple columbine, and gold-veined lilies,
And poppies—sleep in every fold,—
And tangled beds of starry mosses,
And palest bluebells, just unrolled.

O Time, give back to me one little hour
To revel in their sweets again !
Or give me from the myriads one flower—
The dainty star-of-Bethlehem.

APHRODITE.

Under the cool green waves of the sea,
'Neath a starry-blossomed coral tree,
A maiden sat in the dim sea-light ;
Born of the foam ; a fair sea-sprite.
Her beautiful form—of garments bare,
Save her floating vail of dead-gold hair—
Would drive a sculptor to wild despair
With its rounded curves ; its sea-shell flush
Set at defiance Titian's brush.

Her delicate feet the sea-weed pressed ;
Her snowy bosom the waves caressed ;
A sadness (born of a thousand sighs)
Lay in the depths of her dreamy eyes.
She sang, and her words came dreamily,
Like the low, sad murmur of the sea.

"Life passes drearily, drearily,

My heart sighs wearily, wearily,

So impatient am I,

Of the passionate cry

Of my heart.

I tire of the cold sea's caresses,

I tire of the white waves' soft kisses,

No love throb creating,

No answer awaking,

In my heart!"

Then the sea caught up her sad refrain,

And the wild waves echoed it again,

But an idle sea-god heard the song

Of the naiad; heard and listened long.

And as he listened a new desire

Kindled his dark eyes' smouldering fire.

Unfettered he by the ways of men,

Nor waiting for lapse of time, but then,

Through the sea he swam with eager haste,

And clasping the naiad, pure and chaste,

He paused not to ask her yea or nay,

But close to his heart bore her away.

Away down under the purple waves,

With sprays of snowy foam-flowers flecked,

To the rosy dusk of the coral caves,

With tangled garlands of sea-weed decked.

Never again, though they listened long,

Did the wild waves hear the naiad's song.

But sometimes at eve when winds were hushed,

And the sea with sunset fires was flushed,

A thrill of love from the coral caves

Came trembling up through the crimson waves,

And floating out o'er the silent sea,

Was blended with God's eternity.

A PHANTASY.

Above me, high on the canon walls,
The ghostly gleam of the moonlight falls ;
But lower down, the gathering gloom
Shroudeth the night.   The hush of the tomb
Rests o'er the canon ; and, save the flow
Of wild white waves, 't is as silent.   Now,
Along the path by the water side,
Two shadowless figures slowly glide.
A white robe floateth out on the rock ;
Water-sprites, riding the white waves, mock
And laugh, as impassioned whispers fall.
A sudden splash, a smothered call,
Only a dark form stands on the rock.
The wild waves break apart at the shock ;
Foaming, plunging, and flinging their spray ;
Hungrily hiding their passive prey.

A moaning sigh through the tasselled pines,
The scent of the wild rose floats in the air,
A truant moonbeam, quivering, shines
On an upturned face and dead-gold hair,
Framed in a garland of silv'ry spray.
The waters plunge in a mad'ning whirl,
Flinging their glittering drops of pearl,
Bearing their lovely burden away.

As the ling'ring rays of weird moonlight
By gath'ring clouds are overcast,
The vision fadeth out of the night,
Into the mystery-shrouded past.
The mad white stream, the shadowy night,
The dead white face in the wavering light,
A haunting spirit of prophecy,
Will come again, and again, to me.

WE WILL SEEM TO FORGET.

I knew that you loved me, 't were useless to hide it ;
Your eyes told the tale, though your proud lips
  denied it.
I know that you love me ; when your fingers touch
  mine
A thrill of delight that is almost divine
Comes tingling through your finger-tips into mine,
And glows through my frame like a glass of old
  wine.

I know that you love me, by passionate glances
That flash from the shadowy depths of your eyes
Into mine, whenever it happily chances
We meet, and the meeting 's to you a surprise.
Last night when we met in the soft summer star-
  light,

And I knew that we two were alone with the night,

And it chanced our hands met as you gathered a
rose,

Though conscious that duty a faint protest muttered,

Half maddened with love that must never be uttered,

I forgot all the world, and I gathered you close,

Close, close, till your frightened heart throbbed
against mine.

And while we both trembled with rapture divine,

With only the leaves and the shadowy starlight,

And the soft wind that sighed through the dark
tender night,

And the half-sleeping roses to know of our bliss,

I pressed on your lips one long, passionate kiss.

Though your beautiful eyes were soft with love's
languor,

You fled from my arms with well-feigned anger ;

And to-day, when we met on the gay promenade,

You swept coldly by with a slow, haughty grace,
And just bowed with a half-conscious stare in my
    face.

It shall be as you wish ; we will seem to forget
That night, with its roses and soft, tender starlight,
And its beautiful dream of forbidden delight.
Yet I know in your heart you will never forget
That moment of tremulous, rapturous bliss,
When your lips gave to mine that sweet answering
    kiss.

WRITTEN FOR THE LAST DAY OF PRO-
FESSOR W——'S SCHOOL, 1876.

" Knowledge is power "—a truth all must concede,

For 't is the knowledge gained that shapes the deed.

Soon we upon the world's great labor-field

Must enter ; having entered there must yield

Our strength and power to further some good cause.

'T will then behoove us carefully to choose

From all earth's varied labor some vocation

Which native talent, taste, and education

All qualify us best to fill ; but first—

" Know all enjoy that power which suits them best ;

Be sure yourself and your own reach to know,

How far your genius, taste, and learning go ;

Launch not beyond your depth, but be discreet,

And mark that point where sense and dulness meet ;

One science only will one genius fit,
So vast is art, so narrow human wit."

We, who from knowledge's fount have drank so long,
From the same cup must separate ere long,
Life's devious ways diverging paths to tread,
To different works by taste and impulse led.
Some, " young ideas how to shoot," will teach ;
Some into science's boundless depths will reach,
And draw from thence some mighty truths to give
New glory to the age in which they live.
Others, soaring above the mundane sphere,
Time the flight of sunbeams journeying here ;
Or, studying the solar system, trace
The course of star-worlds in their endless race ;
Or, noting when some planet first appears,
Hand down their knowledge to the future years.

And some perhaps into the earth may bore,
And find deep buried there some hidden lore,
That to the world revealed, some light may cast

On the dark ages of the silent past.

While some of us may study nature through

Her winds, her waves, her leaves, her flowers, and
   dew ;

Her singing-birds, that wing the azure air ;

Her oceans, and the beauty hidden there ;

Through e'en the blades of grass that clothe the
   sod :

And they who study thus get nearest God.

Art, science, music, literature, and trade

Shall from our ranks some votaries have made.

But some shall live a life of luxury,

And some shall strive with toil and poverty,

And some a sunny way with roses spread,

And some a clouded, thorny way shall tread.

" Let power or knowledge, gold or glory please,

Or oft more strong than all, the love of ease,"

Make it your rule, where'er your lot is cast,

To act your part with honor to the last ;

That there may be no idle, misspent hours,

To tell, at judgment-day, of wasted powers.

A STORM IN MIDSUMMER.

The winds that have been busily at play
All the long, dreamy, June-embowered day,
Weary of wanton sport among the leaves
Have fallen fast asleep, and lie at rest,
Soft-cradled on the shimmering air,
While prudent silence, finger upon lip,
Creeps everywhere, all nature quieting
Lest weary, sleeping winds should 'wakened be.

The leaves cease whispering, and the grasses
Their emerald lances cease to wave,
The purple harebells still their elfish chimes,
And odorous white lilies passive grow,
Yielding without resistance chaliced sweets
To wandering humming-birds such sweets in quest.

Red, spicy roses, drooping, blush and wait,

While drowsy languor clasps the panting earth,

And holds her in a lingering embrace.

Two hours above the sunset moves the sun,

In golden splendor down the sky's blue west.

Along the horizon low inky banks

Of clouds, each moment growing deeper, lie.

Higher and higher up the azure way

They creep till half in shadow lies the earth.

The fleet-winged swallow, flying swiftly by,

Wheels closer to the ground. From distant woods

Comes plaintively the quail's " Quivet, quivet."

Hark ! through the woods the now awakened wind

Comes rushing. The flowers bend low their heads ;

The green leaves flutter wildly on the boughs,

As it refreshed and cool goes sweeping by ;

Heralding the storm, pausing oft to touch

Caressingly the rustling leaves, and lift

And kiss the blushing faces of the flowers.

Bending the slender trees so low they brush
Against the clover's crimson-tufted bloom,
And twisting, tangling, waving to and fro
The weeping willow's sea-green tresses, till
It seems the spirit of some weird sea-sprite
Has been embodied in the writhing tree.
The pet canary in its gilded cage,
Though not a drop shall damp his yellow coat,
Anoints and plumes his wings and fluffy breast,
Obeying instinct blindly, nature taught.

A sombre veil is drawn across the sky,
Hiding the sunbeams in its dusky folds,
The wind grows chill, and heavy muttered threats
Of distant thunder tremble through the air.
The rain breaks through its filmy prison bars,
And like the pat of thousand fairy feet,
The great drops fall upon the thirsty earth ;
Washing the dusty faces of the leaves,
Swelling the withered petals of the flowers,
Restoring fainting Nature everywhere.

Crash after crash, and fiery lightning flash,

Rends the gray of heaven's vaporous veil.

The rain comes down in torrents, till the roads

Are rivers, and the lawns and gardens, lakes.

At last the storm abates and heaven lifts

Her torn and tattered veil, and through the rifts

The blue and silver of her raiment shines.

The waters in a marvellous way subside,

And tangled sunbeams from the flying clouds

Unwind their glittering threads and earthward

Travel.   Now the whole valley is transformed

Into a picture fair as ever grew

Beneath the magic brush of Claude Lorraine.

The vivid green of vale and hill and wood,

Varied by deeper, ever-changing shades,

Is gilded by the sunset's lingering gold :

With here and there a touch of rosy light,

Caught from the crimson clouds that drift upon

An azure-girdled sea of molten gold

Lifted above the western horizon.

ON THE MOOR.

A lonely house on a lonely moor,
Deserted and silent, stood alone.
The fast-closed gates and the strong-barred door,
Whose hinges and locks were rusty grown,
Had not opened for many a year.
And travellers passed with a sense of fear,
For no sign of human life was there.
The place had a gloomy, haunted air.

In the garden dark and overgrown,
Its silence broken by birds alone,
The ivy over the mossy wall
For years had wandered unmolested.
For years had the roses' bloom and fall
By wanton hand been unarrested.

The marble basin gathering must
Neath the silent fountain empty lay.
The glittering goldfish only dust
Had been for many a summer day.

With every year the shade grew deeper,
And falling leaves and tangled creeper
Quietly covered a loathsome sight :
Under the quaking-aspen's shade,
Where mid-day slept in a dim twilight,
A silken garment but half decayed,
Musty and mildewed by damp and shade,
Mouldering bones and a woman's hair,
Matted and faded, with dark blood stained,
And a gleaming diamond solitaire,
Were all that under the shroud remained ;
The shroud that pitying Nature made.

When the autumn winds are moaning high,
Low bending the purple heather bloom,
A white-robed figure with wailing cry

Glides away in the midnight and gloom
From under the trembling aspen tree.
She cannot rest in her shallow grave,
And so, when the sad winds moan and rave
And dead leaves hold ghostly revelry,
She walks and weeps ; she who was so fair
And frail, with beautiful golden hair.
Unmissed and soon by the world forgot,
If living or dead the world cares not.

But there wanders one beyond the sea
By whom she will ne'er forgotten be.
Two white hands lifted imploringly
For mercy ; two horror-filled eyes upturned,
Their image into his brain have burned.
A phantom follows his steps alway ;
A dead face haunts him by night and day ;
His darkened soul forever oppressed
With a sickening fear—a fear that seems
To take from his life all peace and rest,
Thrilling with horror his very dreams.

He hath sought in revelry to gain
Forgetfulness ; but he seeks in vain.
Though he wanders o'er the world in quest,
His burdened spirit shall find no rest.

The years pass on. "T is the closing hour
Of a golden day by the river Rhine.
The dew lies heavy on leaf and flower,
The mellow sun-steeped fruit of the vine
Purples the slopes of the dreamy hills,
And a flush of crimson lingers still
Above the rim of the western sky.
A perfumed wind with a whispering sigh
Rocks softly in air the drowsy leaves,
The spell that sensuous Nature weaves
Rests on the scene like a dream of love.

At this quiet hour a burdened heart—
No spell of beauty hath power to move,
In whose troubled depths peace hath no part,—
Throbs in the breast of a dying man.

A stricken wretch who with labored breath
Awaits the dreaded approach of Death.
A dark-browed man, wasted and wan,
On a low rude couch in a peasant's cot.
Beside him a woman kneels, whose face,
Of rare dark beauty, still bears the trace,
Though happiness she hath long forgot ;
Though still so young she hath suffered much.

She clasps his hand in her own and weeps ;
Unheeded near her a young child creeps ;
A child who shrank from her father's touch,
While horror stared from her baby eyes.
" Take her away," he cried in despair ;
" I cannot bear the look in her eyes.
The sight of her shining yellow hair
My soul like a rack of torture tries."

He was dying ; could he hope for rest
In death with his dark sin unconfessed ?
He spoke. " You have questioned oft, my wife,

In vain of the past ; of my restless life,

And marvelled my lips were always scaled,

That the past I so jealously concealed.

At last—but remember he who speaks

Is dying ; and in confession seeks

A rest for his soul beyond the tomb.

Genevra, mine is a fearful tale—

O for more light in this gathering gloom !

You shrink from me, tremble, and turn pale.

But promise, whate'er my story be,

Though shrinking, you will not fly from me."

" I will not leave you ; fear not," she said ;

But her heart grew faint with a sickening dread.

The story told none ever knew,

Save that noble woman, brave and true,

Who bound herself with a solemn vow

While the damp of death was on his brow ;

That all that remained of Alean should be

Laid in a grave 'neath the aspen tree.

Time passed on.   On the lonely moor

Two travellers enter the great oak door.

A woman in sombre garments dressed,

And a child with weariness oppressed.

The great door shuts with a grating sound

That echoes through the deserted room.

The woman looks timidly around

The length of the dark hall's eerie gloom.

Beyond the hall through an open door,

A sunbeam through broken shutter strayed ;

Braided its golden threads on the floor,

And by it her weary feet she stayed,

Hushing her weary baby to rest

With tremulous tones, upon her breast.

That night, while her weary baby sleeps,

She stealthily into the garden creeps,

And there on a bed of lilies white

She lays it down in the weird moonlight.

With the aid of a rusty garden spade,

With trembling hands a grave is made,

While a moaning wind the dark boughs wave,

And phantom shadows glide silently
Around her, bending over the grave.
Is it fancy?   In the pale moonlight
A misty figure that moans and weeps
Is bending over the lilies white,
There where her golden-hair'd baby sleeps.
She must not fail though her blood is chilled,
Till her task is done, her vow fulfilled.

While fearful fancies upon her crowd,
With faltering hands she lifts the shroud;
The shroud that pitying Nature weaves,
Of tangled creepers and fallen leaves.
The dust, and jewels, and bleaching bones
In silken shroud in the grave are laid.
A prayer is whispered in solemn tones.
A little mound is over them made;
Then hastily gathered lilies white,
Gleaming with dew in the full moonlight,
Are laid on the grave; a snowy cross
On its cover of emerald moss.

A little later, mother and child
Close fast behind them the great hall door,
And hasten out on the moonlit moor,
Where, safe on a bed of heather wild,
Through the waning night the baby sleeps ;
The mother a sleepless vigil keeps.
Tresses as dark as the starless night
Were hers ere ent'ring that dreaded door ;
But her hair was gleaming snowy white
When the morning sunlight shone once more.

SEA MIST.

Leaning over the great ship's side
I watched the dark'ning waves flow by
With measured rhythm. How dark and wide
The sea, between the land and me !
How drear, I thought, as musingly
I listened to the sea-birds' cry !

Deeper, sweeter, reverently,
I thought of a maiden fair and pale ;
A dainty maid so fanciful,
That every sighing, moaning wail
Of autumn wind would tell a tale
Of direful storms and wrecks at sea.

The night seemed full of tenderness,
The stars shone soft, the wind was still ;

I knew that every hour made less
The dreary, dreary waste of sea—
Bound, as I thought, by time and will—
Stretching between my love and me.

Yet, strange, interminable it seemed.
I felt as one feels who has dreamed
A sad, weird dream, and wakes to find
The pale wraith haunting still his mind.
As if some dark foreboding lay
Upon my heart ; as if the sea—
By some weird Ignis-fatuus led—
Might widen out forever more,
And I, my vague hopes, phantom-fed,
Sail on, and on, eternally ;
Sail on, and never reach the shore.

The moon rose full and white and cold
Above the far-off dusky rim ;
And softly down a silvery flood
Of light fell, lengthening to a road,

Whose whiteness the ship's pathway crossed,
And stretched athwart the throbbing sea.

Against a filmy ray of light
I saw a floating form outlined ;
A woman's form, but pale and dim,
A still, white face, but half defined,
Something familiar, sweet, and fond,
The misty vision seemed to hold.
I saw a dim hand waving me
A last farewell, it seemed ; but why,
I could not tell ; then silently
As the white sea-foam drifting by,
Along the shining road it passed,
Nor faintest line of shadow cast,
Till with the last faint ray 't was lost
In the deep purple gloom beyond.

PROSERPINE.

There by the gray rocks, veined with black moss,
Sun-tinged ; at whose dark, sea-stained feet
The green waves laid their gleaming crests of foam,
She stood upon the dreary, yellow shore.
Above, a leaden sky and clouds wind-blown.
Behind, the dim blue mountains lay outlined
Against the gray ; shrouded in cold, gray mist.
Before her,—murmuring incessantly,—
The solemn, deep, pulsating ocean lay.

She stood there like a statue ; hopelessness
Portrayed in every line of her still face.
Her soft gray robe clinging about her form,
And floating, cloud-like, out upon the sand.
Her hands—whose delicate transparency
Revealed the netted azure underneath ;

Upon whose slender fingers loosely hung
The heavy bands, with flashing jewels set—
Were clasped above her heart, as if to still
Its throbbing.   From her eyes, sad wistfulness
Looked out over old ocean's solitude.
She had gone there for one brief hour, alone,
To lay aside the mask for the world—worn,
And there, alone with God, from whose clear sight
She shrank not to unburden her full heart,
Seek sweet forgetfulness.   The wild sea-gulls
The only living creatures near.   No one
To note her hour of passionate despair.

A little while she stood as in a dream ;
Unmindful of the frown on Nature's face,
Unmindful of the foam-wreathed waves that bore
Their writhing burdens of dark, tangled moss,
And, with sad moaning, laid them on the shore.
Nor mist-veiled mountain, nor wind-driven clouds,
Nor golden sands, nor silver-broidered wave
She saw ; or even the sea-anemones,

Whose violet-veined, fragile beauty lay
So humbly at her feet, close to the sea.
Only the shadow of some hidden grief
That haunted her alway, o'er which her soul
Had brooded through a weary waste of years.

Reaching far out into the empty air,
As if she sought to clasp some fancied form ;
But, finding nothing in her yearning arms,
She sank upon the earth, with one low moan
Of heart-wrung pain ; her frail form quivering
With passionate regret, that madly swept,
Like a great wave of anguish, o'er her soul.
A longing so intense, to feel again
The throbbing of a heart against her own—
The only heart in all the world she prized,
But in whose sunlight Destiny forbade
That she should bask, though she should die for it.

At last she grew more calm, and humbly sought
To woo some comfort from the dreamy realm

Of memory ; a realm whose roses, all
Full-flushed, were braided in with bitter-sweet,
Adown whose purple shore the shadows lay
Entangled in the sunshine's netted gold.
Again she strayed through the oft-trodden paths,
Again the earth was all aglow with love,
And hope's bright bow of promise spanned the
    earth,
And dipped below the misty purple rim.

Again she felt the pressure of warm lips,
Thrilling her into ecstasy.   Again
She read in those dark, shadow-haunted eyes
The love whose sweetness was unutterable.
Then doubt, and fear, and wild despair crept in—
Grim phantoms, turning all her day to night,—
Then sweet, time-mellowed Melancholy sat
In the charmed air, musing forever on
Those sweet lost hours, whose memory the world,
With all its garnered riches, could not buy.
And then a blank of slowly drifting years,

Then came the present, lying hopelessly
In the great shadow of futurity.

The spell is broken and she lifts her head
To find the evening shades are creeping close
Upon the sleeping sea.   The wind is still.
A silence as of death hangs over all.
Rising, she deftly coiled her loosened hair,
And with the subtle touch of practised art
Smoothed out from face and form all trace of grief.
Only the hungry sadness in her eyes—
A sadness deepening with the passing years—
Betrayed her as a few hours later, robed
In costly fabric of a nameless hue,
A spray of creamy roses in her hair
Drooping upon her neck 'gainst rare old lace,
Athrough whose filmy folds rare jewels flashed,
With smile-wreathed lips she mingled with the
      throng
Of pleasure seekers in the gay salon.
Holding with smiles and witty repartee

Her coterie of worshippers ; o'er whom
She reigned alway a fair unrivalled queen.
As woman will, her heart inscrutable
Hiding from all the world's curious eyes.

But in the far, still, veiled hours of night,
Alone and sleepless, brooding o'er her grief,
The voice of her soul's great unuttered want
Despairing cried : " O God ! how long, how long."

THE SEA.

Under the waves, under the waves,
Down in the pink and white coral caves,
What life is so careless and free as ours ?
What beauty so rare as the frail sea-flowers ?
What silence so sweet as silence that loves
The shadowy paths of the coral groves ?
On the soft sea-mosses we lie and dream,
With beautiful serpents that writhe and gleam
When the light comes down through the crystal
    waves
All flushed with the rose of the coral caves.

Down in the sea, down in the sea,
We mermen and maidens hold revelry
When the moon rides high, and the sea is white,

And the pallid rays of the spectral light

Turn into silver the serpent's scales,

As the rosy flush of the coral pales.

But down in the far, still depths of the sea,

We are holding our midnight revelry

When the moon is dark, and the blackest night

Is aglow with the phosphorescent light

Of thousands of curious living lamps.

Where silver'd sea-lilies nod in a dream,

And the emerald eyes of the sea-snakes gleam

As they trail through the slimy cavern damps.

What sailor that saileth over the sea

Would care again to be heart-whole and free,

Or dream of the land when once he has seen,

On a foam-crested wave, a maiden in green,

Flashing love-light from her beautiful eyes,

Heaving her bosom with languorous sighs,

Combing and combing her long shining hair ?

A wily mermaiden, so wondrous fair,

To see is to love, to love is to die,

For false is the light in the mermaiden's eye.

And she combs by day her wildering hair,

Hearts of the honest seamen to ensnare ;

At night, with the mermen down in the sea,

She is holding a midnight revelry.

I COME TO THEE, O NATURE!

I come, O Nature, wounded and weary ;
Wrap me about with thy cool green leaves ;
Lay the sweet spell that thy wild rose weaves,
On my spirit, aweary, aweary !
Let me lie here clinging close to thy breast,
With thy fresh green grasses against my cheek
To cool its burning ; with nothing to break
The beautiful silence of perfect rest,
Save the soothing sound of the whispering trees,
The tremulous notes of the far-away birds,
And a vague, sweet sense of the tender words
Breathed to my soul by the voice of the breeze.

How the world seems fading slowly away ;
The world, with its commonplace cares thatseem

To shut all beauty out from the day—
The day we would set apart for our own,—
Till only the wraith of a broken dream
Is left to us when the day is gone.

Ah me, ah me, there is much of pain,
And little of pleasure, and little to gain
In life that is given to us unasked,
With even its meaning darkly masked !
Fade, fade, O world, with thy tangled web,
With its changing, mocking shadows spread !
If I toiled and toiled till my life should ebb,
I could not unravel its tangled thread.
Press close to my heart, O cool green grasses !
Steal over my senses, O wild-wood flower !
Let tender words of the breeze that passes,
Soothe my tired spirit to rest for an hour.

DREAM ON, YOUNG HEART.

I would not wake you; dream your dream, young
    heart;
Let the sweet spirit of romance impart
Its subtle charm to every hour and day
Of your young life's idealized way.

What though all things on earth are aureoled
With some impalpable radiance of beauty;
What though you fancy that of threads of gold
The shifting webs of sunshine woven be;
That dewdrops on the filmy threads that swing
From briar to bramble and from rose to rose
Across the tangled garden's flowery close
Are jewels set in honor of your waking;
Or that some far-off, vaguely smiling sea
Brings to your feet its priceless argosy.

Dream on, I would not wake you though the noon

Should find you still wrapped in this dream ideal.

For all too soon, alas ! the hour must come,

When imagery is merged into the real.

Must it be so ? must all awake some day

To find their gold but dross, their idols clay ?

HOPE.

To-night, afar down the misty length
Of dim futurity's promised years
I look, and my soul receives new strength.
From out their shadowy depth appears
A vision, distinct, and beautiful.
A vision having a woman's form ;
Majestic, fair, and spiritual.
A lovely woman ; glowing and warm
With life ; never cold and passionless.
She stands on a silver cloud ; the dress
Or floating garment she seems to wear
Appears like a cloud of rosy mist ;
And eternal sunshine's lips have kissed
And left their gold on her waving hair. .
She wears on her regal brow a crown

Of glittering iris, seven-hued.

Her smile is with magical charm imbued.

Her name is Hope ; and all time hath known

The subtle power of her wondrous gift.

On weary mortals, waiting and worn,

She smiles ; and her smile hath power to lift

Or lighten the heavy burden borne.

THE POOR.

O'er our beautiful earth hangs the shadow of death,
And the air hath a taint of the pestilent breath
Of dense-peopled cities ; where want and oppres-
    sion
Are a withering blight on the face of creation.

Our sweet mother Nature with bowed head is weep-
    ing ;
Her children must suffer while Justice is sleeping ;
And the spirit of man is so darkened by crime,
That the black stain may never bleach out in all
    time.

O men of the nation, with wealth-burdened souls,
With hearts that the spirit of Mammon controls,

Go into the discordant precincts of strife,
The foul, crowded alleys, the byways of life ;

Where, hopelessly sinking 'midst poverty's waves,
All burdened with woe, are her myriad slaves ;
Where in damp, filthy cellars, 'mid hunger and cold,
Are children, whose faces are pallid and old ;

Faded, wan women, worn and weary with care ;
And men, who have sought honest labor in vain,
Till their hearts have grown hard, and a prey to
      despair,
They brood o'er their wrongs with a want-weakened
      brain.

Look into the widow's sad, hunger-filled eyes,
As humbly she pleads with gathering tears
For her poor paltry wages, while pitiful cries
Of her half-starving children still ring in her ears.

What wonder that riot and wild insurrection
Should threaten our country with blood-stained
      hand ;

While penury, want, and hopeless starvation,
Like the shadow of death, hang over the land.

Here in the West, 'neath the broad blue of heaven,
Are thousands of life-giving acres untilled ;
Let homes to the poor on this broad earth be
      given,
And the promise of life to mankind be fulfilled.

Let your wealth be the charmed key to the open
      door
Of this garden of plenty to the suffering poor ;
Bring them here, feed and clothe them, till earth
      shall unfold,
Before free, honest labor, her harvest of gold.

LOVE AND PRIMROSES.

It was the time when country lanes are sweet
With apple bloom ; when fields of pale-green wheat
Are deepening in the sun ; when meadow rills
'Tween azure-budded flags go murmuring ;
When lambs lie in the sun upon the hills ;
And maidens dream of love on dusky eves ;
And little wild birds, with soft twittering,
Are building nests amid the tender leaves.

And so it chanced that they two wand'ring went.
She, all on finding primroses intent—
" A yellow primrose by a river's brim."
And he, to pass away an idle hour.
And so they met.   He saw beneath the rim
Of a broad hat a face sweet as a flower,
With eyes that held the light of early dawn.
A rose-bud-sprinkled dress of dainty lawn,

And round white arms, and filmy, ruffled lace,
And little feet that trod with springing grace.
She only saw two eyes, whose dark grey well
Held her rapt glance a moment ere it fell.

By some strange chance, again, and yet again,
They met upon the river's brim, as then.
The river's edge seemed beckoning him alway ;
And her desire for primroses each day
Grew more intense.   But it was in the spring,
And love—sly elf—awake and on the wing,
Ready for instant use, his sharpest dart
Had hidden in a primrose's gold heart.

The autumn woods put on a glow of flame ;
And languorous, indian-summer days,
All golden shod, and wrapped in dim blue haze,
Close following the chilly, gray rains, came.
Perhaps a subtle sense of some past days,
Mayhap a yellow primrose of the spring,
A pale sweet wraith, but dimly vanishing,
Was haunting still two lives.   Ah, who shall say !

A SUMMER PASTIME.

A chance wind bore our barques the same fair way ;
We met as others meet, one summer's day.
We found a wonderously sweet pastime
Exchanging thoughts in prose or subtle rhyme.
His thoughts were brilliant, towards the humorous
    leaning,
And I was quick to catch their hidden meaning.
He liked it, so we two were much together,
Wandering through the pleasant summer weather.

Were there some hidden rocks we could not see,
Or was it but the hand of destiny
That swept our barques apart one dreary day
Farther and farther, till such distance lay
Between us, that our silver-woven dream
Swept shattered into fragments down the stream,

Beyond our reach, beyond ev'n time's recall ;

For should some chance wind that may come to all

Bear our light barques together, even then

We could not find the scattered shining shreds,

Or of the many broken silver threads

Weave whole and fair our summer dream again.

ROBIN.

A little flash of flame 'mid budding boughs,
When winds still breathe of the departed snows.
A cheerful chirping when the early dawn,
Discloses tender green upon the lawn.
O Robin, jewel in the crown of spring,
What joyful tidings to the heart ye bring !
Tidings of soft days of sun and showers,
A sweet foreshadowing of opening flowers,
And faint, far whispers of long dreamy hours
Of languorous summer.   Slow-moving hours
When heaven toward earth bends tenderly,
And earth is still, in rapt expectancy
Of full fruition.   Bird of prophecy,
Teach me thy sweetest lessons in bird lore,
And reign within my heart forevermore.

A MEMORY.

Somewhere adown the charmed purple shore
Of that fair realm that we call memory,
There is a valley ; sunshine shifting o'er
Its grass-rimmed brook continually.
A brook, the azure flag-bloom lingers by,
Where cowslips lave their waxen flowers of gold
In limpid waves, that ripple clear and cold,
Mirroring aye a clear Italian sky.

Upon the bord'ring rim of sunny hills
Are wild crab-apple trees, whose rosy bloom
Drop their pink petals on the grass, until
The very air is languid with perfume.
Above the brook, an overhanging ledge
Its broken wall of granite upward lifts ;

And daisies star the grass along its edge,

And on its side, from out the mossy rifts,

Unfolds the early, pale wood-violet.

The grass—with white and purple daisies set—

Fringes a shadowy place ; quiet, inert,

Where quaint white, rose-flecked lady's-slippers
    grace

Some long-forgotten fairies' spellbound feet.

And brake, and brier, and thorny wild rose sweet,

With wand'ring grape and ivy intertwine.

Where woodland orchis droops its creamy sprays,

And columbine lifts up its crown of flame,

Where silence broods the long midsummer days,—

Hushed days that know no change ; always the
    same.

For in this vale of cherished memory

There is no wintry chill, no autumn blight.

Always the same, its shadows and its light,

And fairest summer reigns eternally.

A KISS.

They had met oft in gay and crowded halls ;
Had danced together oft at fashion's balls ;
But it was chance that led them both that night,
To linger in the garden's shadowy light,
And, loit'ring 'long a path with roses set,
They—all unconscious of each other—met.
By chance they sought to pluck the same red rose,
And plucking this red rose, touched finger-tips.
Then she, its fragrance to inhale, drew close,
And he looked down and thought her ripe, red lips
Were sweeter, temptinger than any rose.
Somehow his arm was 'round her slender waist,
And he was looking deep down in her eyes.
He drew her to him, and with eager haste,
Pressed his warm mouth to hers, O sweet surprise.
Lip clung to lip, and little tingling pains
Of pleasure leapt from throbbing heart to heart.
And now, for that one kiss, till time shall wane,
Their lips must meet, or longing, live apart.

A FRAGMEMT.

---

*   *   *   *   *   *   *   *

Boughs that hung heavy-laden to their tips
With fair white roses, sweet to eyes and lips,
Bent low and becked her.   Ah, God, how sweet !
Scattering their dewy petals at her feet,
As walking on the heights in a half dream,
She saw their snow drift through the silver gleam
Of luminous clouds enfolding her.   Alas !
Their beauty held her soul, she could not pass,
But gathered them until a snowy mass
Of palpitating sweetness lay against her heart.
Then, wide-eyed wonderment, with lips apart,
Beheld her roses change from white to red,
And from their deep hearts such rare fragrance
    shed,

All the rich spices of the Orient
Must, from their fulness, some sweet scent have
  lent.

She breathed their beauty till her spirit lay
In a half trance, through a delicious day
Of sweet, mad dreaming, when the changeful world
Grew beautiful through shim'ring mists of gold,
And fair blue lakes, by mystic mirage held
'Tween heaven and earth, their cool waves swelled,
Till their full sides o'erflowed in crystal streams ;
Cool trickling streams that falling earthward dripped
On shadowy mosses starred with silver gleams
Of milk-white, sweet-breathed lilies, velvet-lipped.
And music whispering through the summer wind,
Soothing with soft lullabies the troubled mind.

Then dreams grew feverish and their sweetness
Changed (she half waking) into bitterness.
Then o'er her spirit a great stillness came,
Hushing all feeling, joy, and pain,

Till pleasure e'en forgot its own sweet name,
And days were ages, and all days the same.

She woke at last to find her hair grown gray,
Her roses hanging dead on every spray,
Their dry brown petals scattered everywhere,
And a sick scent of death in the still air.
She did not mourn her dead, felt no regrets,
The heart that suffers so sometimes forgets.
With listless hands crossed idly on her breast,
And dull, dry eyes she sat, awaiting rest.

A PICTURE.

'I' was night in Naples, and a full-orbed moon
Hung o'er the city. The heart of June,
Heavy with rose and dewy passion-flower,
Laid all its burden on the languid hour ;
And Genevieve wore roses in her hair,
Pink-flushed, love-breathing roses, such as fair
Voluptuous Venus, love's own goddess, wore
After her marvellous creation ; she
Reclining in her sea-shell, floating o'er
A sunlit sea, to charm Olympia.

I cannot paint her dress ; I only know
It was some fabric white as new-born snow,
And mistier than sea-foam drifting o'er
Sea waves of palest green ; and that she wore

A necklace strung of great translucent pearls ;
And that her loosened hair in shining curls
Strayed over her white neck.   Unconsciously,
She stood upon a vine-draped balcony,
Revealed to me by the white moonlight.
Not dreaming that the shadow of the night
Below held one whose charmed wistful eyes
Looked on her beauty ; o'er whose sinful soul
A feeling of sweet, restful calmness stole.

Some tender heart throbs ; some unbidden sighs ;
Well, she will never know.   Time will pass by ;
Wifehood and motherhood be hers ; while I,
I shall live on my feverish mad life
Of dissipation, ignominy, strife.
Perchance a little better for that hour
Of chastening influence, whose subtle power,
Unknown to her, may follow me alway,
Throughout my life's dark, changeful, misspent day.

A SECRET.

I must not tell thee of my love, O Leonore.
The world lies with its worldliness between us.
Long, dreary, empty years must pass before
We two can speak of love together.   Thus

When I look upon that perfect form of thine,
And thy red lips whose kiss must be divine,
And in thine eyes full of a shadowy splendor,
And hear thy voice to me grow low and tender,
And feel thy white hand tremble at my touch,
And thy dark eyes droop shyly 'neath my own,
Believe me 't is because I love so much
That I am silent, purest, sweetest one.

But time will surely bring to us a day
When I may hold thee close against my heart
And tell my love, that I have loved alway,
And loved for all these years we 've been apart.

PETRARCH AND LAURA.

He saw, and seeing loved her ; well, what then,
If he in silent worship stood apart,
Nor looked with covetous eyes, where was the sin ?
Though his rebellious eyes betrayed his heart,
Though his whole being thrilled with ecstasy
If he but touched, in common courtesy,
The rosy satin of her finger-tips ;
So that he never kissed her warm, red lips,
Or held her lovely form pressed close to him,
Or sought to win her love, where was the sin ?
If life and earth grew very beautiful
To him, and he grew tender, pitiful,
Toward all suffering, was it not well ?
If just to love was joy enough for him,
Though his love's sweetness he might never tell
Or ask for a return, where was the sin ?

TIME.

Pause for awhile, O Time, in thy flight,
Ere thou climbest the wearisome height
Of the future, and lighten the years
Of their heavy burden of unshed tears.
What matter it though a few years pass,
And golden sands lie still in thy glass.
What though thou failest to leave a trace
Of age on many a fair young face.
Or failest to weave with silver threads
The crown of hair on beautiful heads.
'T would lift from many a life the cloud
That folds it now like a clinging shroud,
To many a heart that hath not grown old,
The beautiful story of love be told.
I would I might woo thee into a sleep,

Sleep so unconscious, unbroken, and deep,

Thy glass might gather a century's dust ;

The gleaming sickle be dulled with rust.

The dusky folds of thy robe to grasp

I strive ; but powerless my hands unclasp.

Though in wild despair I pray thee stay,

Relentlessly thou dost glide away.

And on, and on, in thy steady flight,

Pausing never, by day or night.

Sowing broadcast—as they sow the grain—

Thorns and roses, pleasure and pain.

Some gather the roses for their part ;

Some bury the thorns deep in their heart.

But onward it must forever be,

'T is vain to repine, 't is God's decree.

A DREAM.

I dreamed that I was standing all alone
Upon a lofty, isolated height.
The moon shone white upon the drifted snow ;
The silent world lay sleeping far below.
Wrapped in some floating drapery of white,
My loosened hair uncovered and wind-blown,
I trod the frozen snow with naked feet
And felt no cold ; alone, I felt no fear.
A silvery mist the sleeping world concealed ;
It seemed a finished volume, closed and sealed.

Above, heaven's deep, illimitable blue,
Gleaming with stars bent tenderly. I knew
That, save my own, no human soul was near,
And felt a sense of freedom strange and sweet.

Some vague, brief glimpses of a higher life,
Too beautiful for human utterance,
Had come to me, like momentary gleams
Of spiritual light.   As some bright dreams,
Vanishing, leave their impress on our life,
So these etherial messengers, that chance,
Or Heaven, had sent me, had awakened long
A deep desire to solve death's mystery.

And now it seemed each moment brought me near
My prayer's fulfilment.   In my mind, a clear
Perception of the truth of right and wrong
Was dawning.   Life, and life's eternity,
To my awakened spirit stood revealed,
A living truth, a joyful certainty,
More beautiful than any dream of heaven,
A gift invaluable to mortal given.
I, who had been so thankless for the gift
Of life always, now humbly knelt to lift
My soul's thanksgiving to my God—revealed
To me through Nature—for creating me.

ICE-BOUND.

Lift, O Spring, the burden of ice and snows,
Weighing so long and heavily on me ;
Benumbing me till low and sluggishly
The thickened current of my being flows.
Press on it the touch of thy soft, warm breath,
Until it melts away in shining drops,
Wrapping with silv'ry mist the mountain tops,
And I be freed once more from living death.

Renew my life with gently falling rain ;
And let me hear the songs of birds again,
And thrill with pleasure when the wild thrush laves
Its plumy breast in my soft, murmuring waves.
Let me but find in the sweet April wind,
The scent of early violets, and I,
If I, O Nature, 'gainst thy laws have sinned,
Ice-bound, will suffer mutely till I die.

HAUNTED.

There came a sound of sobbing through the night ;
A wailing, borne along a wand'ring wind,
As of some troubled spirit that had sinned,
Moaning abroad its woe.   There was no light ;
Not even a far-off star's dim, pallid ray,
Breaking the death dark, closing in on me.
My walk had brought me to a lonely place ;
A lonely place, by weird, hushed whispers set
Apart from others.   Crime and mystery
O'ershadowed it.   A dreary place ; and yet
I paused a moment on the grass-grown walk
To peer above the moldy, blackened wall,
O'er the tall grass, at the deserted hall,
Shut in by its great trees.   Did fancy mock
My senses, or did a pale, ghastly face

Look out from the black, curtainless window?

A sickening sense that I was not alone

Crept over me.   Again that wailing moan

Came trembling on the wind as it swept low

Around the empty house.   Out of the wood

Something came moving slowly through the night.

A dim, white shape, with long hair dripping blood,

With hollow, sunken eyes, whose vacant sight

Seemed not to see me as it glided by.

But as it passed, the weird wind's moaning breath

Shaped into this : "No rest even in death."

Close to the sunken wall a dark pool lay ;

Rimmed in by nettles, and rank smelling weeds ;

Where frogs croaked hoarsely from the slimy reeds.

The stagnant, moveless depths, deep, dark, and
    dead,

Sent up a sickly odor of decay.

Toward this the phantom moved with noiseless
    tread ;

But near the edge, it turned and looked around,

Fixing its hollow eyes on the dark Hall.

Flinging its long arms up, it gave a cry,

Curdling my blood as it pierced through the night,

And died in a long, faint, quivering wail.

The dank weeds parted, but gave out no sound ;

No sound rose as it sank from my strained sight.

The midnight hour, tolled by a distant bell ;

The wind grew still ; a hush was over all.

PHANTASMA.

Through naked branches laced against the sky
In silvery net-work, soft winds whispering by
Promise that to this bleak and dreary clime
Shall come the golden warmth of summer time.
A time of opening buds, of singing birds,
Of dewy moonlit ways, of low love-words.

It cannot bring to me more happiness,
Only a quiet life of usefulness.
And yet I lie and dream, while stealthily
The dusky shades of evening creep
Nearer, until with sudden leap
They meet, and clasp dim hands, and cast
One sombre shadow over me.
The while, I draw from out the past

Long golden threads from mem'ry's sheaves ;

With which my dreamy fancy weaves

A shining web, in which is wrought

The impress of a lovely thought,

A beautiful vague phantasy.

AUTUMN.

Blow, O ye winds of autumn, blow ;
Strip the shivering branches bare ;
Sweep the leaves in a death-whirl low
In drifts ; strike with a dumb despair
The flowers with their limp chilled leaves
And blighted buds, till they shrink and faint
Under a pall of dead, brown leaves.
What is this burden of sad complaint
That is borne on the troubled air ?
Where, O where are the sweet days, where
Are the days when the summer lay
Glowing and still, in rapt content,
And smiled on the bosom of earth ;
Days, when beauty a fulness lent
Unto life and its imagery ;

When her sun-steeped lips, lingeringly
Touched the pulsating, purple sea ?

Close fast my heart, lest thou too be
Stricken low with a dumb despair
Of fear ; lest all joy and light be fled
With the birds, the flowers, and the fair
Sweet dream of the days that are dead.

LINES WRITTEN TO A FRIEND ON THE FIFTIETH ANNIVERSARY OF HER BIRTHDAY.

Fifty years. Can it be that you have known
The sunshine and the storms of fifty years ?
Their roses, and their thorns, their smiles, their
　　tears ?
The years for you with tender grace have flown
To leave so faint an impress of their touch.
Such must the verdict of the world be ; such
A one, I fancy, would have been my own,
Had I not of the many shadows known.

The scanty lines that time hath thought to trace,
But lend a greater charm of earnestness,
Of chastened, kindly feeling to your face ;
A finer shading, deeper thoughtfulness.

Your fair cheeks hold no furrows washed by tears ;
What is the secret of the fleet-winged years ?

You wipe away your tears, that you may smile
And cheer some grief, forgetting yours the while.
You gather up the sunbeams where they lay,
And weave about yourself a halo bright,
And weary-laden ones along your way
Grow stronger in your soul-emitted light.
You pass, unheeded, clouds that threaten you,
Or only see the silver shining through.
What marvel, that the years have left scant trace
Of tears, or hardship, on your sunny face !

A VISION.

Sometimes, on weary nights, there comes to me
A waking dream ; a whispered prophecy ;
A vision, as it seems, of rain-wet woods ;
Of dim, wet woods where restful Silence broods.
Where, through the dripping boughs, the emerald
    gleam
Of shadowy light, soft as a wav'ring dream,
Falls on pale, woodland lilies in the grass ;
That bend to the wet earth as soft winds pass.

Is it a dream, or shall I rest at last
In some still wood forgetful of the past,
Where, 'mid the slender grasses, lilies wave
And scatter snow on my forgotten grave ?
But, whether it be dream or prophecy,
Or but a glimpse of some old memory,
My own, the visions of the woodland are,
And mine the rain-wet lilies growing there.

A NIGHT.

Something in the weird beauty of this night,
In the pale radiance of misty light,
So like unto another night doth seem,
It weighs upon my spirit like a dream.
But whether 't is more sad or sweet, the spell
Holding my soul entranced, I cannot tell.

A night when the white, southern moonlight lay
In silver glory on the silent earth,
And through the parted branches far away,
I saw in the pale sky the marvellous birth
Of spectral lakes, by mystic mirage held
'Twixt heaven and earth.

A FRAGMENT OF A DREAM.

I seemed to stand on some up-lifted height ;
Below me, deep in shadow, cool and dim,
A valley lay.   There in the changeful light
More real than fancied shape of common dream
Leaping from rock to rock with careless grace
Across, a whirling, foaming mountain stream.

Far up above, the snow-crowned furrowed face
Of aged mountains slept against the blue ;
Nearer, below the whispering pine-trees' gloom,
On overhanging rocks, a wild plant grew
From mossy crevices, its crimson bloom
Slow-swinging idly downward in the wind.
A rose that I had fastened in my hair
Fell as I looked, and lay there fresh and sweet
Upon the lichened rocks.

A SUMMER IN DREAM-LAND.

I dreamed in a far, fair summer time,
A dream in whose shadow my soul drifts yet ;
A dream like a poem of perfect rhyme
And rhythm to divinest music set.
In my dream the earth seemed aureoled
With the golden glory of some new light,
In whose radiance beauty seemed to hold
A subtler charm to my soul's rapt sight.
And out of the restless throbbing sea,
And the wind that swept through the lifted leaves,
And the perfume the soul of the flower breathes,
Came voices forever speaking to me.

TO A LOST THOUGHT.

Beautiful, intangible thing,
Just as my mind would grasp thee,
On airy, invisible wing
Thou floatest back to the sea.
Mysterious, unknown sea
Of undefined thought,
From whence thou comest to me
A moment, unsought.

I meant to have made thee mine own,
O fairest, heaven-born thought,
But thy lovely spirit had flown
Ere thy light form I had caught.
Only thy frail shell I find,
Just a feeble impression,
That changing, fades from my mind
Ere I give it expression.

IS THERE A HEART?

Is there a heart but hath within its wall
Some hidden chamber sacred from the rest,
" Holy of holies," where is treasured all
The sweetest memories, the purest, best
Emotions of life's happiest hours ?
Where, is an altar draped with cloth of gold,
With bitter-sweet, and glowing passion-flower,
And roses all enwrought in every fold.
Upon this altar, sacred from all eyes,
In gold and purple bound, the volume lies
Wherein is writ the tenderest memories.
To unlock this book of sweet heart mysteries,
No key, by mortal wrought in quaint design,
Such as ope volumes of forgotten lore,
Possesseth power ; but subtilely each time

Chance fashions one.   In semblance of a flower
Perchance, whose sweetness in some charmed hour
Hath thrilled you with a rapturous delight ;
A strain of some old song, heard in the past ;
Some subtle presence in a summer night
Revealed by the night wind as it passed.
In such strange moulds, the mystic keys are cast,
That ope the treasured volumes of the past.

AN OASIS.

A little while of respite from dull care,
A few brief days of calm, free life, whose fair
Broad walls are hung with pictures framed in air.
Pictures of misty mountain height and ledge ;
Of curving mountain road, whose sunny edge
O'erlooks some deep and shadowy ravine,
Where dark pools mirror the o'erhanging green ;
Of tremulous sighing pines against a sky
With changeful clouds forever floating by ;
Of snow brooks wand'ring fern-fringed rocks be-
    tween ;
A river flowing o'er its rocky bed,
Hurrying, as by some wild impulse led.

And one that is to earthly eyes invisible ;
The voice of the great, Infinite Creation,—
A voice of healing, tender, pitiful,
Giving the weary soul a benediction.

A DREAM.

When southern sunshine smiling lay
In misty gold o'er each charmed way
Of hill, and wood, and valley, set
With bloom of azure violet ;
When 'long the river's sea-green edge
The bloom lay white on wild-thorn hedge,
And red-bud trees a crimson glow put on ;

The swollen river's rapid flow
I lingered on the bridge to see.
And there came drifting down to me
A sweet white rose ; and as it passed—
My soul by some strange spell o'ercast—
I plucked it from its watery bed.
A perfect rose, full, snowy-leaved ;
And from its deep heart flushed with red,
A marvellous, sweet perfume breathed.

WATER-CRESSES.

Water-cresses crisp and tender,
Grown by shady brooks, that wander
Under banks, where weed and wild-rose
Are entangled, growing close ;
With their dark red stems thorn-sprinkled,
With their young leaves, pale and crinkled,
And their promise of pink blossoms
When the flowery May month comes.

Wading through the matted cresses,
With wet feet, and wind-blown tresses,
In the fresh pure air of morning,
To the brim our baskets filling.
Then beside the brook that ripples
Over gleaming sand and pebbles,

Washing lazily our cresses

In the water as it passes,

Murmuring its dreamy measure.

Feeling sure the while, 't is one

Of the spring's most tempting pleasures,

Washing cresses in the sun.

A FRAGMENT.

O River, flowing o'er the sands of time,
Laying your drifting roses at the feet
Of mortals, bringing from some tropic clime
Perchance a sun-born rose, full-flushed and sweet,
To lay its beauty on the ice-bound shore,—
The cold bleak shore of some far northern sea.
Shall thy inscrutable mystery be
To these eyes unrevealed forevermore?

AN IDYL.

We could not wait for her—that loit'rer Spring,—
And so we sought her in her own domains ;
There, found some faint and sweet fore-shadowing
Of her approach, among the charmed mountains.
'Long the willowy margin of the stream,
Where, in the shadow, lines of snow still gleam,
Downy buds on every branch were swelling ;
And in among the rocks on sunny slopes,
Fragrant balm and tender plants were growing.

'Neath shelt'ring banks—fulfilment of our hopes—
We found some " wee sweet blossoms crimson-
 tipped " ;
And as beside a mountain spring we sipped
The cool refreshing nectar, we espied

Some ferns that in the mosses sought to hide
Their tiny coils from our observant eyes.
Later, full-dressed in feathery fringed green
All broidered underneath with russet sheen,
They 'll flaunt their dainty plumes 'neath summer
    skies.

Against a slanting rock we sat and dreamed
Through a still hour that but a moment seemed
In passing ; then above the mountain's brow
Dark clouds looked down on us and mutter'd low
And threatened us and lowering glances set
Upon us. By what right did we invade
The sacred realm of Spring ere she had made
But first faint touches of her toilet.

Beneath those dark'ning clouds we dared not stay,
But bore our spoils triumphantly away
In safety to the broader plains below.
Our spoils, some drooping flowers, some fragrant
    balm,

Some yellow budded sprays, we gathered from

Among the rocks ; within whose every fold

These sweet flowers shone like clustered drops of
gold.

ON THE HEIGHTS.

Let my heaven but be as fair as this,
Where the dark, sighing, moving pine-trees kiss
The clouds that drift upon an azure sky.
Where mingled murmurous sounds and sweet
    winds rock
My spirit in a half dream as I lie
Upon the heights, upon a bed of leaves,
Beneath my head a lichen 'broidered rock,
And that dim purple mountain far away,
Its changeful beauty ever in my sight,—
With undulating foreground, where the play,
The marvellous play of light and shadow weaves
A web whose shifting gold and emerald gives
My dreaming soul a sensuous delight.

SNOW.

Silently it came in the night,
Softly veiling the dim starlight,
Robing the earth with feathery white.
And roof, and fence, and earth, and tree,
Bore each their burden tenderly
Till all was wrapped in mystery.

Morn, awake to the fitness of things,
Put on her pearls and her opal rings,
Brushing with silver her azure wings.
The rising sun in rapt surprise
Flashed rosy gleams from am'rous eyes,
Flinging a veil of gold o'er the skies.

Crowning with gold her shining hair,
Scattering diamonds everywhere,

Eager, he wooed the morning fair.

Yielding she donned the veil of gold ;

A scarf of rose o'er her opals cold,

Paling, paling, as higher rolled

The false sun toward the growing noon,

Fading and dying all too soon ;

Leaving earth as a parting boon,

Her pearls and her opals pale.   And so,

Through each bare, silver-netted bough

The sky wears a film of opal now.

TO A LITTLE BLUE FLOWER.

Only a little blue flower,
Plucked from a mountain's cold brow,
Blossoming close to the snow,
Withered and dead in a hour.
Crisp are thy mossy brown leaves,
Blue as that summer day's sky ;
Thy petals—withered and dry—
But sweet is the rhythm that weaves
Its spell 'round this heart of mine,
As stilly the brown leaves fall,
Whispering me of a time
When fulfilment shall come to all.

TO——

You think you have measured my woman's soul
With your eagle eye ; that the careless glance
You have deigned to cast, has discerned the whole.
You think you have pierced to the very depth
Its clear, silent waters.   You 've seen perchance
On its surface, some water-lilies, or
Some crisp growing cresses, whose pungence keeps
Your fancy a moment, and nothing more
Beneath, save the shallowest bed of sand.
You little dream that there are depths that might try
The power of your keen, far-seeing eye
To fathom ; and so you throw me a smile—
A smile you might give to a winsome child ;
Or in flippant badinage you beguile
The passing away of an idle hour.

But the moments passed you have thus beguiled,

You thrust me aside, as a child might cast

A toy it had wearied of at last.

And you shut me out from your thoughts so grand

And deep, thinking I could not understand ;

Nor know, through the fragile flowery growth,

That floats on its surface, my soul looks forth

From its beautiful underworld at you,

And searches you, and reads you through and
    through.

But beyond all this there must come a day

When our souls as an open book must lay

To be read and understood ; and you

Will know me at last, as I know you now.

WRITTEN FOR THE LAST DAY OF PRO-FESSOR W——'S SCHOOL, FOR THE THIRD DEPARTMENT. MOTTO ON THE BANNER : "UPWARD AND ON-WARD."

We stand to-day upon the lower rounds

Of the endless ladder of progression.

Looking below, how few the rounds appear

Whereon our feet have rested, in the years

Of our brief lives, now but a memory.

Above, round after round, the ladder rears

Its height beyond our reach of vision,

Through unknown realms of dim eternity.

But we will not despond, though knowledge fill,

In varied forms, such vast immensity ;

Though the steep height that we must climb extends

Through time's eternity.   Life is eternal.

Youth, health, are ours ; our motive-power, am-
 bition ;
While hope's bright bow of promise o'er us bends,
Clasping with shining arch, futurity.
We will have nobly done if we have found,
Each year, a foothold on a higher round.
" Upward and Onward " let our motto be.
Success will crown our efforts, if we will
With perseverance labor to the end.

LET ME ALONE.

Let me alone. The petty cares you bring
But mar the beauty of this perfect day,
And vex my spirit with their scent of clay.
Just to lie here and watch the leaves that swing
Above, sun-silvered, in the grand old trees,
In ceaseless tremulous motion in the breeze
That passes freighted with the breath of flowers,
Is all I ask for, in this hour of hours.

No one hath right to know my thoughts as I
Lie here and feel the silvery gray-blue sky
Looking with tender softness down on me,
Sensing the wind's light kisses dreamily
Upon my loosened hair. And if the leaves
Thrill more intensely reading them, what then ?

Or if the rose, whose sweets my soul receives

Glows deeper red at some sweet thought of mine,

What then ? Thought is the soul's rightful heritage,

And only He from whence it comes may hold

The book of records, on whose fairest page

Our purest thoughts are writ in words of gold.

A NOVEMBER SUNSET.

I saw the sun sink slowly down the west
'Gainst a pale purple sky ;
Until he rested like a glittering crest
Upon a wave of gold
That, one of thousands, 'rose out of a sea
That, like a pale mirage,
Clasped the dim horizon.   A moment, and
He sank ; and I could hear
The plash of broken waves closing o'er him.

A rosy flush crept up the purple arch
And broke in crimson clouds
With luminous, fiery edges.   Silent lay
The Earth, with bated breath,
Watching the glory of the sunset fires ;

'Waiting some revelation.

Through sombre brown of branch and leaf

I caught the rosy gleam

Of sunset-lighted windows ; and I thought,

That cunning artist, Nature,

Just touched them with his magic brush

To make the picture perfect.

MIDSUMMER.

The fleecy cotton from the trees,
Like snow-flakes through the summer air,
Floats listless, on an idle breeze.
'Mid drowsy leaves, that scarcely stir,
The orioles flit in and out ;
In black, with scarf of orange dressed,
Coquetting, with their bills close-pressed,
They flutter fearlessly about.

Everywhere, on roof and gate,
The pigeon, with love-softened coos,
All plumed in purple, bowing, woos
Persistently his soft-eyed mate.
And so the summer day goes by ;
And summer winds, with languorous sigh,

Go with the sun to rest ; while I,

With senses wandering dreamily,

Look longingly toward fairy-land ;

Where distant mountains, purple-veiled,

Wear kingly crowns of misty gold,

A crimson flush in every fold :

Where sunset's rosy garments trailed,

In passing by to fairy-land.

LINES WRITTEN IN A FRIEND'S ALBUM.

Hew off the roughness ; let the gem shine forth ;
But not as it with fitful lustre now
The earthly incrustations gleameth through,
But pure and bright, and from all rubbish free,
That all the world its native brilliancy
May see, and seeing, know of its great worth.

DRIFTING LEAVES.

There is a silv'ry light on the flowing river,
Save in dusky lines where tree shadows quiver ;
And wave voices whisper, " Forever, ever,"
Through the hours of the still summer night.

Over there in shadow-land, close to the brink,
A pale, wind-waved lily bends over to drink ;
And blue, elfin violets sleepingly wink,
In the summer night's wavering light.

Two leaflets—from tremulous branches wafted—
Together falling, by light winds are lifted,
And rocked in a dream, down the river drifted,
Farther, and farther, till out of sight.

Would I, like those leaves, on the swift-flowing
    river,
The pulsating breast of the moonlit river,
Forgot, and forgetting, might drift forever,
Throughout an eternal summer night.

SLEEP.

I feel your fingers, O gentle Sleep,
Pressing my languorous eyelids down,
And softly over my senses creep
Forgetfulness, till the world hath grown
Less real than the vague, approaching dream,
For dreams are more real than they seem.

GROWING OLD (A REVERY).

Is it because the storm to-day
Hath gathered low its clouds of gray
'Twixt earth and sky,
And ceaselessly the falling rain
Hath beat against the window pane
With fitful sigh,

That hope, whose bright alluring gleam
Hath made so real my life's sweet dream,
Grows dim and pale ;
And down the future's shadowy years,
Seen through a sombre mist of tears,
I hear the wail

Of a soul that moans a useless life,
Of wasted time, and toil, and strife,

Seeking for fame,—
Fame, the reward for good deeds done
To man, for evils overcome,
A world-known name.

Fame, and the world's homage, for me,
A fantasy could only be.
Vain fool am I
To harbor in my heart a hope
For fame ; with greater minds to cope.
I 've soared too high

On fancy's wing ; and now, forsooth,
I must content me with the truth,
And curb ambition ;
Truth stripped of the garment thin,
Delusive hope hath clothed it in,
For its brief mission.

Ere I can hope to win one leaf,
Fresh from fame's golden laurel wreath,

To crown my brow,
Many a deep, long, earnest draught,
From knowledge's fountain slowly quaffed,
My life must know.

Years of arduous toil must pass ;
I shall be growing old.   Alas !
Alas ! e'en now
Long silver threads gleam here and there
Through the thick darkness of my hair,
About my brow.

Ere I can grasp her changeful light,
My life will reach its dim twilight,
Be almost o'er ;
I, drifting down the shadowy stream,
Weary of life's feverish dream,
Close to the other shore.